D0723276

A MAN CALLED SAVAGE

In New York, an agent hired by the head of the Pinkerton agency would gain the respect of any law-breaker. But is Allan Pinkerton mistaken with this baby-faced killer named Savage? His task: to break up two gangs terrorizing the south-west. Armed with a shotgun — and his concealed knife — he must infiltrate and destroy both gangs, a seemingly impossible mission. Can he justify Pinkerton's faith, or will he die of lead poisoning?

Books by Sydney J. Bounds
in the Linford Western Library:

SAVAGE'S FEUD

SYDNEY J. BOUNDS

A MAN CALLED SAVAGE

Complete and Unabridged

LINFORD
Leicester

First published in Great Britain in 2000

First Linford Edition
published 2007

The moral right of the author has been asserted

British Library CIP Data

Bounds, Sydney J.
  A man called Savage.—Large print ed.—
  Linford western library
  1. Western stories
  2. Large type books
  I. Title
  823.9′14 [F]

  ISBN 978–1–84617–812–2

Published by
F. A. Thorpe (Publishing)
Anstey, Leicestershire

Set by Words & Graphics Ltd.
Anstey, Leicestershire
Printed and bound in Great Britain by
T. J. International Ltd., Padstow, Cornwall

This book is printed on acid-free paper

1

He rode the Southern Pacific into town. The train shuddered to a halt with a hiss of expelled steam and clanking couplings. As his coach finally stopped jolting, the young man who had taken the name of Savage roused himself from a corner seat to peer through a grimy window.

The depot lay under a layer of white dust and the noon sun filled the air with a fierce light. He squinted, warily studying the town. Fremont was no New York, but at least it had the buildings and traffic and the bustle of people going about their business; a welcome sight after days of nothing but flat open space.

Most of his fury had burned out during the long disjointed journey across the continent from north-east to south-west, changing from one railroad to another. He felt now only a dull resentment at being used.

He stared at a line of men waiting on the platform, men openly carrying guns — maybe one of them was Edsel — and thought: this won't do. He made a conscious effort to sharpen his wits and focus his attention. His life could depend on being alert.

He opened the valise on the seat beside him, took out a long-bladed kitchen knife and thrust it into his belt. Then he set his derby to a rakish angle and stepped down from the coach, a short wiry figure in black broadcloth and low-heeled boots. His frilled cambric shirt was creased after more travelling than he'd previously done in his nineteen years.

No-one appeared to be waiting to meet him, so he started to walk down Main Street, valise swinging in his left hand. The street was wide and dusty but not quite what he'd imagined from his reading of dime novels; a vivid memory popped up of rescuing a coverless *Scouts of the Plains* from a garbage dump. Fremont was a county seat now, but the evidence of what it had grown from was still clear.

He passed saloons and cattlemen in store suits, women shopping with kids, a red brick courthouse; a billiards parlour, barber's-shop and hotel proclaiming itself to be the *Miner's Rest*. He kept walking, stubbornly refusing to ask his way. Signs advertised a stage company, gunshop and the best food in town. He heard a Southern drawl and smelled fried chicken. Wagons churned up the acrid dust in thick clouds.

His chalk-pale skin contrasted with the wind-and-sun burned tan of those about him. He reached a crossroads with a saloon on one corner and a laundry opposite; across the road was a store and the *Southwest and Border Bank*. There was a sign above the side door of the bank:

PINKERTON AGENCY
TERRITORIAL SUPERVISOR

He climbed narrow wooden stairs to a small office that had the door and window wide open. A middle-aged man in shirt sleeves sat at a desk littered with papers. The walls were plastered with WANTED notices. A revolver in a shoulder holster hung from a peg, and sounds and smells and dust drifted up from the street.

'Mr Edsel?'

'Yeah. What can I do for you?'

Edsel had a tough-looking face, an experienced expression about his hooded eyes. His skin was walnut-wrinkled, his bushy hair touched with grey and superfluous weight sagged around his waist.

'My name's Savage.'

Edsel pushed back his chair and lifted one eyebrow as he studied the new operative. He saw a baby-face, with blue eyes and straw-coloured hair.

'Waal now, take a seat. And tell me why Mister Allan would send me a raw Yankee kid?'

Savage placed his valise on the floor and sat down and bit his tongue to hold back the reply: If I told yuh, you wouldn't like it! He needed Edsel for local information and as back-up man; there was no advantage in upsetting him.

The Pinkerton supervisor shuffled papers and waved a telegraph form. 'Been expecting yuh.' He read it again, folded the form and tucked it away. He wiped the dust from a couple of glasses and lifted a bottle from a niche in his desk.

'Guess you'll need a drink to lay this dust.'

'Not for me. I never touch the stuff.'

Edsel raised his other eyebrow, then nodded. 'Wise. Use a gun, do yuh?'

Savage shook his head, touched the haft of his knife with his right hand.

Edsel looked doubtful. 'Ride a horse?'

'No.'

'Out here, you'll need range clothes.' The Pinkerton man sighed in resignation. 'Gawd, everything. You know what you're getting into? Being a Yankee, the rebs'll eat you alive.'

'They can try . . . I want a wash and a meal. Your boss said you'd advance me expenses.'

Edsel winced, rose and unlocked a metal safe in the corner, counted a handful of notes and coins onto the desk-top. 'You understand this has to be accounted for? Every cent — in writing — and don't forget it.'

Savage scooped up the money and shoved it in his pocket, and moved for the door. 'See you.'

He clattered down the stairs, whistling; money, just like that, for the asking. On the street he moved along jauntily, swinging his valise, to the *Miner's Rest*. He turned into the hotel and walked up to the desk.

'I want a room, a bath, and a meal.'

'Yes sir. Will you sign the register, please?'

Savage signed with a flourish, took the key and went upstairs. His room overlooked Main and, from the window, he noticed a hand-lettered sign on a shop front opposite:

J. WEBSTER
PHOTOGRAPHIC STUDIO

He luxuriated in a tub of hot water, changed into a fresh shirt, brushed the dust from his suit and descended to the dining room. He filled on T-bone steak with extra vegetables, apple-pie with cream and two large cups of coffee. New York was never like this . . .

Refreshed, he collected his valise, settled the hotel bill and strolled across the street. The photographs in the studio window were well done and showed aspects of life in the West: cowboys roping a steer, one trying to ride a wild horse, another using a branding iron.

A gaunt man in a smock appeared in the doorway. He had a heavy beard, a nose too large for his face, and his eyes bulged like the eyes of a fish.

'Jonathan Webster at your service, sir.'

'Savage.' He gestured at the window display. 'Interesting stuff. I suppose you move around a lot?'

'Just so, sir.' Webster's voice was dour. 'I'm making a tour of the western territories, travelling from the Mississippi to California, to capture frontier life on plate. This will form a historical record for the future. I intend to give exhibitions to make my name and, hopefully, some money.'

The gaunt face framed a bleak smile.

'Say, John — '

'Jonathan, if you don't mind.'

' . . . Jonathan. In your travels, I bet you pick up all sorts of information. You'll have heard if there are gangs of outlaws operating in this area.'

'One can hardly help hearing such things. A rapacious mob by all accounts.'

'Have you heard anything recently? Like where they might be right now?'

Webster shrugged. 'The reports are conflicting. They are here, they are there — they might be anywhere. Personally I hope never to meet up with them. Not that they would profit much by stopping me.'

'Hard times, huh?'

'I find that folk are reluctant to part with money for my western studies, so I take portraits to pay my way. If you wish, Mister Savage, I can take yours now. My fee is fifty cents.'

'Yeah, why not?'

Savage stepped through the doorway. The studio was a single large bare room smelling of chemicals; it contained a sink and a bench littered with cameras and plates and trays. He felt good, proud of his new clothes.

'If you'll sit here . . . '

The high-backed chair faced a large camera on a tripod. Savage sat, solemn-faced.

Jonathan Webster disappeared beneath a black cloth.

'Hold quite still please. This takes a little time.'

Savage held his breath and a strained smile. The wait seemed to go on and on . . .

'All right. Thank you.'

As Webster reappeared, Savage rose

and fished out fifty cents.

'I may not be able to collect it myself. Leave it with Edsel the Pinkerton agent, if I'm not around.'

He ambled out, strolled along Main to the *Southwest and Border Bank*.

In his office at the top of the stairs, Edsel looked as if he hadn't stirred from his desk as he sat dealing with a pile of paper forms. But Savage noticed a shotgun with its barrel sawn off standing in the corner, and a canvas pack beside it.

The Pinkerton supervisor leaned back in the chair and knuckled his eyes.

'The curse of this job, paperwork. But more times than not, it's the routine that eventually leads to the men we're after. This time is an exception.'

He stood up and hefted the shotgun, broke the barrel and pushed in two shells, closed it again.

'There's nothing to it, you see? Just point the weapon and pull the triggers. And remember it's a close range gun.'

He tossed the shotgun and Savage caught it.

'You've probably heard a lot of rubbish talked about cowboys shooting off their pistols? Discount it. Maybe one of 'em could hit a barn door, but I wouldn't put any money on it. A professional gunfighter now, that's a different matter. That's why I'm giving yuh this — a scatter gun scares hell even out of a professional.'

Edsel hitched up his belt.

'There's food in the pack, water canteen and a blanket. Your starting point will be Calico — small place, used to be some mining there, but it's pretty dead now. Rumour says it's the closest town to wherever it is the gangs have their hideout . . . let's get down to the livery. I want you out of town before too many eyes see us together.'

Savage collected his pack and valise and hefted it downstairs and along Main. He could smell horses before Edsel turned into the stable through a big double door. There were buggies for hire and horses in individual stalls. A man using a curry-comb paused and called:

'Hi there, Mister Edsel. Do something for yuh?'

'Man of mine needs a horse. A quiet number with plenty of stamina.'

'Sure thing. Take a look at the black.'

Edsel walked around a big stallion, pinching and poking. 'Yeah, should do. Put it on the agency account.'

He helped himself to a saddle and blanket and showed Savage how to adjust the stirrups and tighten the cinches. 'You'll soon get used to it.'

He lashed the pack and shotgun behind the saddle. 'Waal, next thing's some clothes.'

'No,' Savage said. 'I just bought this outfit and I'm sticking to it.'

Edsel peered at his face. 'Your choice.'

He took the reins and walked the black down Main to the edge of town. 'Let's see you mount up.'

Savage placed a foot in one stirrup,

grasped the saddlehorn with both hands and heaved himself up. Awkwardly he threw a leg over the horse's back and fumbled for the far stirrup.

Edsel raised eyes to the sky and murmured, 'Gawd, help him, please . . . well, at least the horse didn't bolt, is something.'

He kept hold of the reins as Savage wriggled about, trying to get comfortable in the saddle.

'Follow the trail west and you should hit Calico. If you get lost, give the horse his head and he'll take you to water. You look after him, he'll see you through. And report back, you hear me?'

'I hear you.'

Edsel slapped the black's rump with the flat of his hand and the horse moved forward at a stately walk. Savage tried to hold the reins and the saddlehorn at the same time as he adjusted to the swaying motion. He'd get used to it in time, he told himself. There was no hurry.

The trail was a dust track across open

land. The sun, a dusky red ball in the sky before him, was the only aiming point, and he tilted his derby forward to shield his eyes. He was alone, surrounded by a plain of parched grass and rocky outcrops, with no sign of human habitation ahead or to right or left.

He turned in the saddle to look back as the stallion plodded on. Fremont was a purple shadow on the horizon, vanishing small.

'Let's see how far we can get before dark, Horse.'

He shook the reins and the black broke into a trot. As he jogged along, Savage's thoughts reverted to his old life . . .

2

A chill mist curled in lazy shreds about the water-front on New York's East Side. A blood-red sun, easing up from the horizon, managed a glimmer of light but no warmth. Cranes loomed like metal skeletons. Water slapped at the creaking piles of the piers and the sound covered the stealthy padding of feet.

He shivered in thin and ragged clothes as he darted across the dock-yard. He was hungry, but something could soon be done about that — providing he wasn't caught. His left hand clutched a hempen sack containing coffee beans stolen from the hold of one of the newly-berthed freighters in harbour.

There was only one idea in his head; to exchange his loot for a hot meal. His parents had been immigrants to the New World, poor and not in the best of

15

health. Since they had died, he'd become a loner fending for himself.

His right hand rested lightly on the handle of a long-bladed kitchen knife thrust through the belt holding up his threadbare pants. He was ready to fight if he had to, and it wasn't any thought of the police that bothered him.

A rat scurried away. There were the mingled smells of fish and brine and tar. A bell-buoy clanged mournfully, and shadowed figures loomed out of the mist to form a barrier across his path.

He paused, peering intently, counting the opposition and trying to identify the leader of the gang. There were dock thieves who preyed on their own kind.

He recognized their leader, a hulking figure who carried a massive iron wrench.

'Hi, short-ass,' Bull called. 'Let's see what you've got in the sack. We'll take our share — and for that, you get protection. Okay?'

He drew his knife, teeth bared,

poised on the balls of his feet. 'Just stay away from me.'

Bull scowled. 'Drop it, kid! Any trouble, and I'll break both your arms.' He swung the heavy wrench threateningly.

He moved with the smoothness and suddenness of a cat, the knife lunging forward. Bull jumped back, late and cursing as blood poured from a long gash in his arm. The wrench dropped from his hand.

'Jesus, the little bastard cut me! Get 'im!'

The gang closed in, circling, clubs swinging. A weighted cosh numbed his left arm and the hempen sack fell from nerveless fingers.

It was a silent vicious fight. He managed to keep them at a distance with savage sweeps of his blade, but he was outnumbered and they kept crowding him.

Bull snatched up his wrench, holding it one-handed. 'Hold 'im still — I'm goin' to bash his skull in!'

He snarled like a cornered tiger as they surrounded him, and sprang forward, his knife arrowing for Bull's broad chest. It was a target he couldn't miss. The blade went in cleanly — he felt it sink into solid flesh, grate on bone, and then slide between the ribs — and when he jerked it out it was stained red.

Bull staggered back, sagging at the knees, and collapsed in a heap.

The gang froze.

'Gawd, 'e's killed Bull!'

He recovered his balance and went into the attack, knife slashing wildly. He cut one of them, and they turned and fled into the mist.

For a long moment he stood poised, listening intently to the fading clatter of boots. He was panting from his exertions.

He glanced at the body on the ground, then moved round it to recover his sack of beans. As he bent over to pick it up, silent figures moved out of the mist behind him.

He heard the unmistakable clicking of guns being cocked and straightened up fast, whirling about to see pistols aimed at his head and body.

'Drop the knife,' a brusque voice demanded.

He stood still, poised for flight or attack, studying faces and positions, looking for a way out. These men — in hard-worn business suits — looked neither like police nor dockside thieves.

'Who are you?'

'Pinkerton detectives.'

Three revolvers pointed at him, held rock steady in experienced hands. They weren't about to rush him, or allow him within slashing distance.

There was no chance at all for the moment. He resisted an impulse to fight uselessly, made himself relax, and allowed the knife to slip from his hand.

'Intelligent,' commented the man with bushy whiskers. 'Now, you're coming with us, and without trouble. Mister Allan wants to talk to you.'

The detective motioned to the man

on his left. 'Get rid of the body.'

'Okay, Dave.'

The Pinkerton man grabbed the body by the ankles, dragged it to the edge of the pier and rolled it over. It sank with a splash.

'The cops aren't going to worry about a missing dock rat,' Dave said. 'Unless we tell 'em.' He picked up the bloody knife, wiped the blade and thrust it through his belt. 'Right, let's move it.'

The Pinkerton men opened a way for him to walk between them, then closed ranks, guns handy. Together they left the pier and walked along an alley to the cobble-stoned highway where a horse-drawn cab waited.

One detective got inside, then Savage — reluctantly — then a second agent. He sat between them, guns poking into his ribs. Dave snapped handcuffs on him.

He glowered in silence, noting which pocket the key was slipped into.

Dave chuckled. 'Don't try it, kid!'

The cab jerked forward, moving past brothels and boarding-houses and grogshops. The sour reek of a tannery permeated the atmosphere. The dawn light showed the blank brick walls of warehouses.

Up-town, the buildings rose higher and the streets filled up with early workmen, horse-drawn trolleys, wagons and carts loaded with farm produce.

The cab drove on till it arrived at a part of the city he was not familiar with, and drew up outside an office block.

'Out,' Dave said tersely. 'And if you want your knife back, be good.'

He was hustled into the building, along a corridor to a door with a sign:

PINKERTON DETECTIVE AGENCY
WE NEVER SLEEP

The office beyond was large and airy. There was a roll-top desk, oak-panelled walls, a telephone on the wall and shelves of cardboard files.

An oldish man, bearded, stood with hands behind his back, looking out of

21

the window. He turned leisurely, studied him with sharp eyes, silent.

After a minute he said: 'Take the cuffs off, and leave us.'

'Don't take any chances with him,' Dave warned. 'He's a young savage.'

Pinkerton smiled grimly. 'Is he now? Remove the cuffs, please.'

Dave shrugged, took the key from his pocket and unlocked the handcuffs.

He massaged his wrists, said: 'I want my knife back.'

'No weapons,' Pinkerton ordered. 'Take a seat — we have something to discuss. Would you care for a drink? A cigar?'

'I'm hungry.'

Pinkerton sat down at his desk. 'Breakfast for two,' he said, and the ops left.

'What name do I call you by?'

'Savage is as good as any.' He took a chair opposite.

Pinkerton's eyes gleamed. 'I like that. Very well, Mr Savage. I've been looking for somebody like you for a job I want done. A tough job. I've had a man watching you for a while now — he reports that you're a loner, fast on your feet and self-reliant. Apparently you've never been arrested, are an expert with a knife and reasonably intelligent.'

He paused to stroke his beard. 'I should, by rights, hand you over to the authorities but, in my opinion, that would be a waste of potentially useful material. So I'm offering you a choice, the opportunity to go straight and work on the side of law and order — or take a prison sentence.'

The door opened and a detective brought in a tray with a white cloth over it. He moved a side table up to the desk, set down the tray and removed the cloth. Under it were two large plates piled with bacon and sausages and fried potatoes, thick wedges of bread and two mugs of steaming coffee.

Savage didn't wait to be invited; he helped himself to a plate and ate greedily.

The detective passed Pinkerton a

note before he left the office. The head of the agency read it, glanced at Savage, then began to eat too. After a few minutes, he asked: 'Are you listening, Mister Savage?'

He nodded. 'What's the job?'

'The job is out west. South-west, to be exact.' Pinkerton left his desk and moved to a large-scale map pinned to the wall. His finger traced an inked line close to the US-Mexican border. 'This line represents the trail west used by stages, emigrants, cattlemen and miners. Homesteaders and farmers are settling along the route and opening up the land for further development. Ordinary hard-working people. This country needs those people out there.'

He sat down again before continuing.

Savage listened with one ear, mopping up the last morsel on his plate with a hunk of bread.

'Unfortunately there are gangs of outlaws — two major gangs we know of and possibly others involved — who prey on those using the trail. Vicious gangs who don't stop at robbing those travelling in coaches and wagons. They rape women and murder the men — even children are not safe. They make their raids and then retreat to some hideout we haven't been able to find.'

Savage sipped his coffee, strong, black and sweet, and listened.

'The country is such — wild and largely uninhabited — that these gangs are not readily apprehended. Not that lawmen are in great numbers in the area. It is essential to locate their hideout — only then will it be possible to mount a posse to deal with these outlaws.'

Savage looked at the wall-map. There didn't appear to be anything much along the inked-in trail.

'This route must be made safe for people moving west. The governor of the territory has approached me — in effect, commanded me — to locate their hideout, to identify the gangs preying on innocent travellers and to smash them utterly.'

Savage put down his empty mug. 'Why me?'

'I have one permanent agent in the area. He is known, of course. I could move agents in from other areas but, frankly, I think they'd be obvious for what they are — and I need an undercover man. I'm gambling that an East Side dock thief is tougher than any western outlaw and able to beat them at their own game. Well?' Pinkerton looked calmly at him. 'It's your choice. I can hand you over to the police — ' He glanced at the note his detective had handed to him and his voice grew harsh. ' — but now the charge will be one of murder! Or you can go out West and work for me. Which is it to be?'

Savage scowled. The law wasn't about to take a light-hearted view of murder — but he hated being pushed into a corner.

He stared sullenly at Allan Pinkerton.

'All right,' he said savagely. 'You don't give me much choice, do you? I'll do what you want.'

3

The land was flat and featureless to every horizon. It was an arid land, the grass scorched brown, the earth hard and powdery. Just how hard Savage learnt the first night out, when he tried to sleep with his saddle for a pillow and a single blanket around him.

A scattering of scrubby vegetation, mainly cacti, struggled to exist and, without his horse, he would neither have kept to the trail nor found water.

Sweat soaked him and his skin was red raw where it was exposed to the direct rays of the sun. The sky was a deep blue bowl, cloudless. The insides of his thighs were sore from jogging in the saddle, the air oven-hot and dry, with not the slightest breeze to alleviate it. His clothes were covered in fine white dust.

The landscape remained empty of

life, desolate, even the rocks weathered down to mere humps. Savage allowed the black to find its way at its own pace; he had quickly learnt that without his horse he was a dead man. His throat was parched but he refused to allow himself to drink the few remaining drops of water in his canteen till the horse located more. Instead, he chewed on a strip of dried beef.

He knew himself to be a natural loner, but the loneliness of this land was frightening. Who would want it anyway? He'd read of mirages and refused to believe that the smudge on the forward horizon could really be a town.

Since leaving Fremont he had practised regularly with the shotgun till he was satisfied he could operate it efficiently; but he was almost out of shells. Remembering New York was like imagining another life, remote and dream-like; how proud he'd been to go into a tailor's shop with the money Pinkerton had given him and buy a suit and shirts and a derby hat. Then setting off by train to cross a continent to meet Edsel, the local superintendent.

He slumped in the saddle, all the resentment burnt out of him, as the black plodded on, until it registered that the distant smudge was not an illusion; that there really was a small town ahead and that it could only be Calico.

He straightened up, flicked the reins to encourage his horse to break into a trot. Shading his eyes from the sun, he saw buildings grouped about a crossroads, and he was glad to see them. Tonight he would sleep in a bed.

A small creek ran just outside the town and he paused to let the black drink its fill, then sluiced warm water over his face and moistened his cracked lips and throat. His awareness sharpened. Calico was close to outlaw territory and men meant danger, particularly here.

The trail, dusty and wide, became obvious as wooden and adobe shacks sprang up on either side; most appeared to be empty and neglected. Doors hung open. Neither were there many people on the street as he passed the stage and freight office, a restaurant, a two-storey hotel, a couple of saloons.

On a corner of the crossroads was the largest building in town, proclaiming itself to be the *Crystal Palace*. The few loungers on the board-walk regarded him with curiosity as he rode past.

On the opposite corner sprawled a general store bearing the name HOPPER. There was a carpenter's shop, butcher's, another saloon. The whole place looked run-down. *Rooms-to-let* signs in windows were old and tatty. A tall cottonwood grew outside the marshal's office. Marshal? No-one had mentioned any law in Calico . . .

There was a buckboard and a few horses tethered to a hitching rail, a dog lying in the shade, tongue lolling. He rode the length of Main Street, watching the smirks on weathered faces, hearing ribald comments.

'A greenhorn!'

'Some fancy dude, huh?'

The sun was beginning to set and loafers gathered as he reached a fenced corral and barn with the faded sign, LIVERY AND SMITHY, and dismounted and led his horse inside.

A man with a lame leg limped towards him from the dark interior.

'Look after him,' Savage said as he stripped his gear from his weary mount.

'Sure, mister. I'll feed him corn.'

Men gathered in sunlight at the wide-open double doors. A Southern drawl asked: 'Y' all see what I see?'

A hate-filled voice answered: 'Reckon it's a Yankee bastard!'

A tall skinny man spat on Savage as he turned to face the gathering crowd, hand closing on the hilt of his knife. His muscles tightened up.

'You ain't wanted here, kid,' the skinny man said.

'Don't call me *kid!*'

Savage moved fast, tiredness sloughing from him. His knife jerked from his belt, slashed wildly at the man's face.

The skinny man stumbled back, a thin red line marking him. His voice came out scared, 'Jesus, he's crazy!'

The loafers backed away. The red sunlight of evening slanted into the barn; the silence was filled with the smell of horses and greased leather. The crippled liveryman kept well in the background.

Savage waited, grinning, blade held low.

A newcomer pushed his way through the half-circle of onlookers. He was a squat man, bow-legged, with thick black curly hair and a star pinned to his chest. He carried a revolver in his hand.

His voice was hard as he rapped: 'Cut that out, stranger.'

Savage's instinct was to go into the attack. He paused, recalling that he was now supposed to be on the side of the law — and this man had to be the town marshal. He counted to three to give himself time to relax; after all, it was possible the marshal could provide him with information.

'Anyone picks a fight with me, they get just that. You call them off.'

The marshal held his gun steady on him. 'My name's Bick and I run this town my way. You thinking of staying?'

Savage pushed his knife down into his belt. 'Could be, Marshal, that I'll be staying. Depends.'

Bick studied him closely, then holstered his Colt with a curt nod.

'That's for the mayor to decide. If he allows you to stay . . . otherwise I run you out, and don't think I can't.'

Savage stared at him in disbelief, then made a gesture to encompass the dirt street, the wood shacks and mud walls.

'Mayor? Of this one-horse dump?' His voice mirrored his incredulity. 'Who is this bigshot?'

' 'Name's Garrison, feller, and he calls all the shots around here. As you'll find out if you rub him the wrong way.'

'Yeah?' Savage decided not to lean any harder until he'd learnt more about the set-up in Calico. 'I suggest you tell your Mister Garrison that I'm here and I just might be staying.'

He turned his back on the marshal, picked up his shotgun and valise. 'Going to find me a room and a place to eat,' he told the liveryman.

'Yes sir.'

Savage walked up Main Street, watched by Bick and a silent crowd of loafers. The skinny man he'd cut seemed to have disappeared. He went into the hotel and up to the desk.

'Need a room and bath.'

The hotelman was small with a sly, weasel face. 'Staying long?'

'Could be.'

'That'll be five dollars in advance.'

Savage shrugged and paid, took the key and carried his gear upstairs. The place was quiet, his room stuffy. He opened the window and looked out; lights were coming on in the saloons and a piano tinkled. The sun was half of a red ball dropping below the horizon.

He bathed and changed his shirt and walked along the street to the dining rooms. A middle-aged woman in an apron looked sharply at him.

'It's hash and biscuits and coffee — that's all I've got left.'

'Just serve it up.'

He sat watching the empty street till his meal arrived, then ate ravenously, mopping up thick gravy with the last of his biscuits. The coffee was black and strong.

'Nice cooking, ma'am.'

'I'm the only cook in town, so you'd better get used to it.'

He paid and, in the twilight, walked back past the hotel. There might be some night life, and he wanted to get to know the layout in the dark. Passing the *Crystal Palace*, a woman's voice hailed him and he looked up.

She was leaning from the window of an upper storey, a buxom blonde in a dressing gown that gaped to expose breasts bulging over the top of her corset to the cool evening air. She was, perhaps, twenty-five, but to Savage she looked good and he immediately felt randy.

'Five bucks,' she called. 'Why don't yuh come up and see the elephant?'

He bared his teeth in a smile; it was Pinkerton's money. 'The trunk looks good — why not?'

'Through the saloon — I'll meet yuh at the top of the stairs. I'm Anna.'

He entered the *Crystal Palace* which was almost empty so early in the evening. Behind the long bar was a line of mirrors, dusty and reflecting the room so it seemed twice as wide. Chandeliers hung from the ceiling. At the far end, a few men sat playing cards; one was the skinny man, his face marked with a livid scar. When he saw Savage he whispered something to the man next to him.

Savage ignored them and went up the worn, carpeted stairs. Anna waited for him on the landing, a big smile on the rouged and powdered mask that was her face.

'In here.'

Her room was big enough for a double-bed, a small table with a wash-basin and an oil-stove. A kettle boiled on the stove. The room was hot, the window open. The bed sagged from overuse and the red plush curtains had lost their nap. Her scent nearly overpowered him.

'You don't have to worry, kid — I'm clean.'

'Just don't call me kid,' he said, irritated.

'Okay. What do I call yuh?'

'Savage.'

She opened her gown and he saw she'd got rid of the corset. All she was wearing were black stockings held up by fancy garters, and paste earrings. She kicked off her mules and lay back on the bed with her legs spread wide.

Staring at her, Savage licked dry lips and wrestled with stiff buttons. He dropped his pants and climbed onto her. Her arms went around him, holding him tightly, nipples digging into his chest as, panting, he entered her.

When he'd finished, she rolled over and reached for a cigarette, lit up and blew smoke at the ceiling.

'No need to rush away,' she said. 'I'll make coffee. There's not many in town tonight, and I appreciate a young one.'

She slipped into her mules and padded to the stove. 'Where you from? . . . if you don't mind me asking?' she added hastily.

'New York. Things got a bit hot for me. Guess I'll stay a while, till trouble blows over. No-one back east is going to waste time looking for me out here.'

He accepted a mug of coffee, made room for her on the bed. 'Hear tell there's outlaw gangs operating some-place near.'

Anna grimaced. 'You want to stay away from them hombres. They're poison.'

'Yeah?'

'Yeah.' She looked intently into his face. 'Real mean, kill yuh as soon as look at yuh.'

Savage smiled coldly. 'I don't kill that easy, Anna. Tell me more.'

'The Preacher's the worst,' she said

with a shudder. 'When he holds up a stage or wagon, he murders whole families, including the kids. So there ain't no witness, see? And he always rapes the women before he kills 'em, like it was his trademark. He's got a real big outfit — so I hear.'

'You hear a lot.'

'I'm saying too much.' There was fear in her voice.

Savage put down his mug and fondled her.

'You don't have to worry — I don't repeat what people tell me. Who else is there?'

'There's Kelly, of course.' Anna sniffed. 'A woman. A woman with brain enough to run a gang of men — but she's still a killer.'

She crushed out her cigarette. 'You ready?'

'Guess so . . . maybe it'll be fun hiding out.'

'Depends what Garrison says.'

'Yeah? Seems to me Mister Garrison has a whole lot to say about the way things are run in this town. Maybe it's time I met him.'

Anna rolled onto her back. 'Garrison can wait — I can't.'

4

West of Calico, where the trail left the plain and began the long climb towards wooded hills, there was an outcrop of weathered rock. The formation made a small oasis, irregular and multi-coloured rocks providing shadow for men to sprawl at their ease. Water bubbled slowly from an underground spring, supporting enough grass for a few horses to graze.

One man lay atop the highest peak, exposed to the sun's glare and watching the trail. Below, a hard-case crew smoked and played cards, glancing up from time to time at the look-out, impatiently awaiting his signal.

But none was harder than the Preacher. Despite intense heat, he wore his long black coat buttoned tightly across his chest, a cartridge belt and holstered Colt .45 outside. Wisps of greying hair straggled from beneath a black flat-crowned hat. He appeared a skeletal figure as he stalked back and forth, reading the Good Book. His skin was drawn finely over a skull-face, his expression was as stone and his eyes slitted.

He was the only man there who did not show signs of impatience as he waited. The others moved restlessly and grumbled among themselves.

'Stage sure is late.'

'So? As long as there's gold aboard, who cares?'

'If there is . . . '

'Maybe there'll be women travelling this trip.'

The Preacher's gaze flicked towards his men. He felt deep satisfaction — to be feared gave him the only real gratification he knew these days — but there were moments when he despised the tools he used.

'Patience is a Godly virtue,' he intoned softly. 'As is silence. Desist from grumbling lest the wrath of the Lord visit ye.'

Big Mal grinned. The Preacher's second-in-command was bear-sized with an ugly face and the brute strength of a natural bully.

'You heard the man,' he said. 'Quiet now.'

The gang fell silent; every man was a killer and wanted by the law, yet there was not one who did not fear their leader.

Mal looked at a long-haired lanky man smoking a cheroot. 'You, Cash — get up there and relieve Luke.'

Cash squeezed out his cheroot and picked up a Sharps rifle, checked it was loaded and scrambled to the top of the rock. Luke nodded and went down, in a hurry to get in the shade and take a cool drink.

Cash lay flat atop the hot rock, hat tilted to shade his eyes as he watched the trail. He levered a shell into place and took sight on a known mark.

The western trail had provided good picking for the gang. Wagons still came — sod-busters never seemed to learn

43

— but stages were less frequent. And the rumour of gold made him itchy to get his hands on it.

He waited, motionless, under a burning sun.

Presently dust rose in a cloud on the horizon; someone was coming. Cash sighted carefully and curled a finger round the trigger of his Sharps, waiting for his target to get within range.

He called down: 'Stage coming!'

Below, men dropped cards and cigarettes and reached for guns.

The Preacher shouted up: 'Drop the lead horse.'

'Sure thing.'

The gang crouched behind rocks close to the trail, hidden and waiting like vultures for their prey . . .

The coach rattled along at a fair clip pulled by a team of four, dust churning from beneath the wheels and springs creaking. The driver cracked his whip above the heads of the lead horses.

Gramp was an old-timer, walnut-wrinkled and weather-shrivelled, and had been saving his horses for this stretch; now he wanted their best speed.

On the box-seat beside him, young Chet allowed a hand-rolled cigarette to dangle from his bottom lip as he made a production out of handling his shotgun. He was young enough to fancy himself in the role of hero.

'Think they've heard we're carrying gold, Gramp?'

'Hoping they haven't,' the driver answered, urging his team to greater effort as they hit the upward slope.

'Yeah? Waal, me, I'm hoping to take a shot at these hombres. Smart though, dropping word we're carrying bullion — while all the time it goes secretly by another route. Yeah, smart.'

'Just keep your eyes peeled and that gun pointing away from me,' Gramp said tersely.

In his opinion, Chet was too cocky by far. There was only one way to find out if the youngster would stand up under fire, and he wasn't keen on learning the hard way.

There were four passengers inside the swaying coach. The man in the corner seat, facing forward, wore a city suit and had slender and supple fingers. Slim Jacobs, gambler by inclination, was heading out to California to see if he could mine gold the easy way. A cool man, his dark coat was open and he carried a derringer in a shoulder holster.

He admired — discreetly — the woman sitting opposite him. In her early thirties, he judged, with a mature figure filling a plain dress. The kind of woman to give a man the feeling that marriage and settling down to raise a family wasn't such a bad notion after all.

She was holding hands with her husband, a solid man in equally plain clothes and farmer written all over him. Their son, about five, was over-excited and fidgety.

He jumped up on the seat to look out of the window.

'Will we be held up, Pa?'

It was the woman, perspiring freely, who spoke. 'Sit down, Daniel, and stop annoying Mr Jacobs.'

'He's no bother, ma'am,' Slim said easily.

William Kent held a Colt revolver in his fist, and his fist made it look a toy. He was looking forward to the challenge of breaking new ground and starting again from scratch, and was ready to defend his family if need be.

'It is worrying,' Sophie, his wife, said.

'I reckon naught . . . '

As the stage approached the rocky outcrop, a single shot, like the crack of a whip, stabbed the air and the lead nearside horse stumbled and fell, dragging down the other ones with it. Leather, strained beyond endurance, snapped; the coach lurched and tilted, crashed down on its side, wheels spinning uselessly.

Cries of alarm came from inside. Gramp sailed through the air to land on his head and lay half-stunned. Chet jumped and landed on his feet, gripping his shotgun. He was still looking for the outlaws when a rifle bullet went through his stomach and mushroomed out, shattering his spine. He fell, hands over his belly, screaming.

As the Preacher's gang closed in, gunfire erupted from the overturned coach. But the attackers had all the advantage; they kept moving while the passengers were pinned down.

The Preacher, Colt in one hand and Bible in the other, boomed: 'Repent, for ye are about to meet thy Maker!' He detected movement as Gramp stirred on the ground. His .45 blasted and the old-timer's jaw disintegrated.

The outlaws ran in, guns firing continuously, riddling the wooden framework of the coach. Splinters flew; curses rang out.

William Kent, one side of his head bloody, stood up in the window, pointing his revolver. A hailstorm of lead hurled him backwards.

Inside, Slim Jacobs dropped his now empty derringer and picked up the Colt. He remained cool even though he knew he had no chance.

He placed the muzzle to a crack in the timber and fired steadily. He wanted to take at least one of them with him . . . it was his last thought as three slugs exploded his heart.

Sophie Kent was living a nightmare. She knew only that she had to get away. She crawled out of the coach, clutching her son.

Big Mal picked her up with one hand and clubbed her with a massive fist and dropped her senseless in the dust. Daniel screamed and tried to rouse his mother. Mal shot him and kicked the body to one side.

The gunfire ended and in the silence, horses threshed and whinnied, trying to rise. Chet whimpered, 'I'm hurt . . . hurt . . . ' till one of the outlaws put him out of his misery.

Two bodies were dragged out.

'Sure hope you ain't killed the woman, Mal,' Luke said. He was small and bow-legged and not popular on account of his smell. 'She's a looker.'

'Naw, she's only stunned.'

Cash descended to join the gang. 'Where's the gold? he asked.

The wrecked coach was searched; mail sacks contained only mail. There was no bullion.

Cash spat in disgust. 'Hell, this is a waste of time.'

The outlaw stripped and searched the bodies, looting them of wallets and watches, anything that could be converted into money.

The Preacher turned his attention to the woman, the one passenger left alive. In her early thirties, he judged, with a well-developed figure. He used his boot to roll her over and emptied his canteen into her face.

Sophie spluttered and sat up, staring blankly about her. She saw the body of her son and screamed, 'You dirty murdering bastards!'

As she struggled to rise, the Preacher backhanded her across the mouth, knocking her down again.

'Silence, woman. The servants of the Lord require thy services.'

Sophie started to crawl towards Daniel's corpse.

'Hold the godless cow,' the Preacher commanded, and two men wrestled her onto her back and pinioned her arms.

Sophie screamed and the Preacher smiled as he saw fear register in her face. One by one, all the members of the outlaw gang used her to relieve their tension until she was numbed flesh, even her moans stifled to a whimper.

The Preacher looked down with satisfaction. 'Now ye are stripped of pride, daughter. Repent, before it is too late.' He drew his Colt, pointed it at her belly and squeezed the trigger.

He supervised the sharing of the loot among his followers and they swung into their saddles and rode away.

For perhaps half-an-hour they rode in silence, into the hills. Higher up, a stream watered the land and grass grew and stunted trees bordered the winding trail. They rode leisurely under a hot sun, sure in the knowledge that there would be no pursuit.

Presently, Cash lit a cheroot and addressed the air. 'Sure's a pity there was no gold.'

Mal's ugly face frowned at him. 'Feller who passed us that word will get his head busted.'

'Even so, that don't put money in my pocket.'

The Preacher turned on their discontent in a voice like thunder.

'Gold? Let me not hear talk of avarice. The Lord has provided a woman, and is not a woman worth more than rubies? It shall come to pass, if He chooses, that ye shall prosper.'

Cash rode on in silence, smoking, thinking that no woman was worth a hatful of gold, but he didn't voice his thoughts aloud. That would be dangerous in the Preacher's current mood.

Mountains loomed ahead and the land split as if cloven by a giant's axe. Watered by small creeks, cedars grew tall, masking the entrance to a narrow canyon. They rode between high rock walls and came to a fertile valley.

5

Savage slept late. When he woke the sun was a blinding light beyond the dusty window. He washed, dressed with care and went out for breakfast.

Refreshed, he strolled along the boardwalk to the livery, knife thrust through his belt and derby set to its usual angle. The lame man was shoeing a horse when he walked in.

There was the pungent smell of burning hair, the fiery glare of the forge, the ringing blows of a hammer as he shaped red-hot iron into a shoe. The 'smith plunged the metal into a bucket of water and looked round.

'Your horse is fine, mister. Wiped him down and fed him corn. He's raring to go when you are.'

'I ain't going anyplace just yet.'

'Didn't mean it that way.'

Savage looked over the black stallion

and decided he must be part-way to becoming a westerner; he'd learnt that his horse was next in importance to his life.

'Your leg don't hold you back much,' he commented.

'Got kicked by a horse, broke a bone and it didn't set right. I manage.'

'You Garrison's man?'

The smith weighed the hammer in his hand, and spat. 'My name's Robson and I'm my own man. There ain't many of us in Calico, but I'm one. What's that to you?'

'Just curious.'

A wary look came to Robson's eyes. Despite solid shoulders and a stubborn jaw, his voice lowered and his words were carefully chosen.

'I'm the only 'smith in these parts. Garrison leaves me alone, and I don't mess in his business. You'll ride away — I live here.'

'I take your point, Mister Robson.'

Savage went outside and headed back towards the *Crystal Palace*; it was time to meet Garrison. The sun was hot, the air dry and, even on the boardwalk, dust soon covered his boots.

He passed the marshal's office, closed, and the only tree in town — a tall cottonwood. He ignored the stares of idlers outside Hopper's store and crossed West Street. The *Crystal Palace* was almost empty, a lone barman wiped down the counter before a solitary drinker. Four others sat at a corner table playing poker, a couple of men stood behind them. At one time the saloon had held a certain glamour; now it appeared run-down and going to seed.

Skinny sat at a piano, handmade cigarette hanging from his bottom lip, tinkling 'Oh! Susanna' on the ivories.

Savage approached the counter. 'I'm looking for Garrison.'

'Mister Garrison to you.' The barman jerked a thumb to indicate the card players.

Savage eased across the room, straddled a chair and watched the game. One of the players was Marshal Bick.

Only one man could be Garrison. He was fiftyish and solidly built, his white hair trimmed short, with a bristle-brush moustache. His suit was obviously expensive; a gold watch-chain straddled his vest, gold earrings and fat rings on his fingers caught the light. He looked satisfied with himself and his way of life.

He had a bottle beside him, from his own private stock, and a cigar between manicured fingers. He was well-fed and well looked after.

The mayor of Calico flicked a glance his way as he laid a card. His grey eyes held no hint of a smile. 'We sell drinks here,' he said in a Southern drawl.

'I don't drink.'

Behind Savage, Skinny interrupted his tune with a dramatic chord.

'Take a hand of cards then.'

'I don't gamble either.'

Another chord sounded.

'You stay long and you'll put me out

of business. I prefer big spenders. Why don't you just drift along?'

'Hear tell you own this town,' Savage said softly. 'So I reckon I should apply to you. Some men back east are hunting me, and I'm looking for a hideaway for a time.'

Garrison played another card. 'Then maybe I should ask the marshal to arrest you.'

Savage shrugged carelessly. 'That's up to you — he's your marshal.'

Bick glowered in silence. Skinny pounded out another chord.

'D'you have any money?'

'Enough to pay my way till I find my feet.'

Garrison nodded absently. 'Maybe I can help. No promises. We'll see.' He gave all his attention to the game.

Savage studied the saloon. The room was long and wide and had been well-appointed at an earlier time. Now the gilt was peeling from the framed mirrors and the oil paintings of buxom nudes were masked by a patina of dirt.

He looked at the two men standing behind the mayor. Both wore gun-belts and deputy badges.

Garrison said, 'My hand,' and scooped the money on the table towards him.

Savage put a snarl into his voice. 'Figure you're the big man around here? Back east, you'd be very small beer!'

'Figure you're just a punk kid still wet behind the ears.'

'Don't call me kid!' Savage shouted, rising from his chair and drawing his knife.

Miraculously, a small derringer seemed to grow from Garrison's hand. Down his sleeve, Savage surmised, staring into the large bore.

'Take a walk, kid.'

Skinny played a fistful of chords, slow and loud. He laughed as Savage took a deep breath, turned and cat-footed to the batwing.

Outside, the sun roasted Savage as he crossed diagonally and stepped into the shade of Hopper's Hardware and General Store.

The interior was far larger than it appeared from outside; the building went far back and was divided into sections. He guessed that at some time barns and outbuildings had been joined to the main building.

There were shelves filled with canned peaches, and crackers, and bacon. Racks of shirts and Levi pants, boots and hats; spades and axes; harness equipment; guns and knives.

Savage studied the storekeeper, a stout man somewhere between thirty and forty, with a ruddy face and bushy side whiskers.

'Do something for yuh?' Mark Hopper asked.

'Looking for shotgun shells.'

Hopper brought up a box from beneath the counter. 'Two dollars to you.'

Savage guessed he was being over-charged but it wasn't his money and, anyway, Hopper had monopoly. There was nowhere else to go.

'I'll take half-a-dozen boxes.'

He looked over the knives and his eyes glistened; they were beauties, the kind he could appreciate. He withdrew one from its sheath; long and razor sharp with a horn handle.

'That's a genuine Bowie,' Hopper said.

'I'll take it.'

Savage stalked past barrels of flour and coffee, a counter stacked with tobacco, to look at a range of wide-brimmed hats. He remembered his long ride from Fremont and finally admitted to himself that a derby just wasn't suitable for this country.

He tried on Stetsons till he found one that fitted. 'What's the total?'

Hopper's eyes lighted and he licked his lips as Savage counted out bills and gold pieces and asked, 'You own this place?'

'Naw, I run it for Garrison.'

'Sure seems like he owns the whole town.'

'You'd better believe it, stranger.'

'I'm beginning to.'

When Savage stepped outside and looked along Main, at the deserted and derelict shacks, he wondered: how could the town support a store that size? Why did Hopper — read Garrison — carry so much stock, much of it perishable?

He was in a thoughtful mood as he carried his purchases back to the hotel. He climbed the stairs to his room, opened the window and looked out. The town was quiet, just a few idlers dozing on a bench in the shade.

He loaded his shotgun and propped it next to the bed, removed his hat and coat and stretched out, the knife close to his hand.

The next move was up to Garrison, so he relaxed, content to wait. And if he were going to revisit Anna — she seemed his best source for information — he'd better get some sleep.

He catnapped, then washed and descended to the hall. Weasel-face was at the desk, and Savage paused.

'You own this dump?' he asked.

'I manage it for Mr Garrison. Name's Kramer. Why, you got a complaint?'

'Just curious.'

Savage went out onto the street, watched by Kramer's sly eyes. He strolled along to the dining rooms. The middle-aged woman was alone when he entered.

'Steak, if you've got it,' he said, taking a window seat.

'One steak coming up.'

He sat studying the street, lights coming on in saloon windows, drifters moving through the shadows. The smell of frying meat suddenly made his mouth water and he looked around. The tables were plain, their tops scrubbed clean, the chairs straight-backed, the door into the kitchen wide open.

When his meal was served, he said, 'Smells good.'

The woman smiled, and looked years younger. 'My customers usually come back.'

'Been in Calico long?'

'Since the boom. That's finished now — the mines are shut.'

'Sounds like a difficult time.'

'Yeah, but I manage to stay alive. Just.'

'Garrison own this place?'

'No, he don't! I'm my own woman.'

'One of the few, I guess.'

'Yeah. I'm called Gin — short for Virginia, not booze. Garrison likes his food and I'm a good cook, so he leaves me alone.' She wiped her hands on her apron. 'Take a tip, son. You don't go speaking agin Garrison in this town — not if you want to go on living.'

Savage bared his teeth and touched the hilt of his knife. 'I can take care of Garrison or anyone else.'

She looked at him, muttered something under her breath and retreated to the kitchen.

Savage finished his meal, lingering over a mug of coffee. He felt relaxed and confident. He left money for his meal, set the new Stetson proudly atop his head, stepped out into the dark and eased along to the *Crystal Palace*.

Oil lamps flared, pushing back the shadows. He thrust past the batwings and paused a moment; it was noisy tonight, Skinny at the piano, several card games going, men drinking at the bar, some of the girls from upstairs soliciting custom.

As he crossed to the stairs he saw Garrison and Bick together, watching him, Hopper joined them. On the landing at the top, Anna waited, her face anxious.

'What's up?' he asked.

She pulled him into her room and shut the door. 'Be extra careful — Garrison's suspicious of you.'

'I'm just another paying customer.'

Anna shook her head. 'He's asked me to spy on you — see what I can find out.'

Savage shrugged. 'So tell him what he wants to hear.'

As he undressed, she threw off her gown and lay back on the bed.

'Listen will you? I've taken a fancy to yuh. For Gawd's sake take me seriously — don't trust him.'

'I don't trust anyone,' Savage told her bluntly.

6

The early morning sun shone over a barren plain and a bunch of riders. As the town of Fremont appeared on the horizon, their leader lifted a hand and reined back.

Kelly waited in silence for her riders to gather round. She was a big-boned woman who looked older than her thirty years. She wore skin-tight Levis over broad hips and a man's shirt lay open at the neck to reveal the divide between full breasts. Long red hair was tied back and tinted dust-grey from the ride. She was plain-featured apart from amber eyes that gleamed with a lust for reckless living. Her dark skin, heritage of an Indian mother, was studded with freckles passed down from her Irish father.

While she studied the faces of her gang, she lit a cheroot and inhaled deeply.

Juan, her lieutenant, fancied himself as a Latin romeo. Slim as a beanpole with a pencil-line moustache, he wore dark ornamented with silver, sombrero, and guns with fancy inlaid butts. But his eyes were the give-away; they were mean eyes.

Griff was solid brawn, a tough fighter with rock-hard fists and completely loyal to her. Rafe was a freed slave with gleaming white teeth in his bald head. All the others were hard men, stubble-chinned, and carried an assortment of artillery. It irked Kelly that they carried so many weapons. Although she was a dead-shot with the .44 Winchester booted at her saddle, she relied on her brains to run the gang and plan her robberies. And her men respected her, for she was a cold-blooded killer when necessary.

'I'm not going over it again. We're hitting the bank at the crossroads and you know what to do. If you've got any doubts or questions, now's the time to air them.'

Juan had been chafing at the bit.

'Por Dios, you should let me lead the raid. You make the plan — you have the brain, we all admit it. But a hombre should lead men, a man with a gun. And I am the best!'

'I'm leading,' Kelly said curtly. 'You Mexes are too hot-blooded. If any little thing goes wrong, you start using a gun instead of your head.'

She looked round the ring of eager faces. 'That it?'

There were no further comments.

Kelly threw her cheroot away, said, 'Let's ride,' and dug spurs into the flanks of her horse.

'And remember, no shootings. We want hard cash, not lead!'

The gang split up to approach the town from different directions. Kelly rode with Griff. The big man remained silent; she always felt more comfortable with him than with any other man in her outfit.

They slowed their horses to a walk to enter the outskirts of Fremont. The town was quiet. They passed the stables and reached the crossroads. A wagon was loading up outside the store across the way from the South-west and Border Bank. As they dismounted and she tied her reins to the store's hitching rail, Kelly studied the layout.

The doors of the bank stood wide open and it was obvious there were few customers inside. She didn't think they'd be expecting a raid this early in the morning. The one bank guard, just inside the door, was yawning.

She glanced up at the window above, knowing it housed the local Pinkerton agent. From what her spies told her, he was not likely to make trouble; he was getting past it, a manager who stuck with the paperwork and left the action to others. There was no sign of him at that moment.

She mounted the boardwalk and paused to watch Juan ride down the street, two men with him. They hitched outside a saloon opposite the bank.

Griff waited with the horses while she

went into the store and cast an eye over bolts of cloth. Through the window she saw Rafe and the rest of the gang drift into town, riding casually; they dismounted outside the Chinese laundry.

Everyone was in place with no suspicion aroused. She stepped outside and nodded to Griff. They crossed the wide dusty street, no-one taking much notice of them, went up three steps and in through the door.

Griff was a fraction in the lead, Kelly lagging, watching from the corner of her eye as the horse-holder carefully moved their horses nearer, ready for the getaway. Juan, Rafe and the others approached casually along the boardwalk on each side.

Just inside the door Kelly paused fractionally to place the customers — three men — the two bank clerks and the armed guard. Griff was close to the guard.

Deliberately she pulled her shirt out from her waist-belt, opened the front wide and pulled back.

She called in a loud voice: 'Hi, fellers. Take a good look and tell me if you've ever seen a better pair.'

Male heads turned, staring at her as she posed naked to the waist, shoulders back and sun freckled breasts thrust forward. Every man in the bank was hooked.

'My man complains they ain't big enough for him. What d'you reckon?'

Every eye was riveted on her. Men held their breath, gaping. For vital seconds she was the centre of attention.

No-one noticed when Griff felled the guard with a massive fist and took charge of his shotgun. Then the rest of the gang burst through the door, guns in their hands.

Kelly said briskly, 'Show's over, fellas. Nobody gets heroic, nobody gets hurt. Just ante up.'

She buttoned her shirt and accepted a rifle from Juan.

The two clerks, one wearing steel-framed spectacles and the other a green eye-shade, were slow on the uptake, still dazed. They gawked at her until Kelly stepped up to the solid wood counter and pushed the muzzle of her rifle under their noses.

'You can lose more than money,' she said coldly. 'Move it!'

The two clerks reluctantly shovelled notes and silver coins across the counter where eager hands thrust it into canvas sacks.

Kelly strolled to the door, aware of the strong scent of wax polish. She looked out at the street, in both directions. There was no sign of excitement. She gave a hand-signal and the holder brought their horses up to the door.

'Okay,' she called back. 'Get going.'

One by one the gang moved out, each carrying a sack, and vaulted into the saddle. Kelly was the last to leave, her rifle swinging to cover both clerks and customers.

'No-one moves, no-one shouts. Just freeze right where you stand.'

One customer, an old man, cackled,

'Call again any time, lady!'

Kelly went through the door and sprang into her saddle. 'Let's ride.'

They spurred their horses and swept down Main at a gallop. Behind them, a man ran from the bank, shouting, 'Robbers!'

Kelly held her rifle in both hands, reins slack, gripping with tight-pressed knees to her horse's flanks. Soon lead would be flying. She leaned forward as she raced along the street, raising a cloud of dust.

'Keep going!'

A shot crashed out . . .

Edsel had the window wide open to get some air into his tiny office above the *South-west and Border Bank*. He sat at his desk in morning sunlight, regarding a pile of paperwork without enthusiasm.

Vague street sounds drifted up to him; the town appeared busier than usual for the time of day.

He took a bottle from his desk and poured himself a drink. I must be getting old, he thought, just don't seem able to face the day's chores without a drink.

He took a slow swallow, then drained the glass, idly wondering if young Savage was still alive. He still couldn't figure why head office had sent a Yankee kid against the gangs; he didn't stand a hope in Hell. Edsel didn't expect anything to come of it, didn't expect to hear from him again.

Likely enough the kid was lying dead someplace right now. A gunshot startled him out of his reverie. He jumped up, knocking over the empty glass, and looked out of the window.

He saw men running from the bank carrying sacks, leap on to horses and gallop away down Main. A hold-up, and right under his nose. Cursing, Edsel snatched up his gun-belt and, still buckling it, pounded down the stairs to the street.

A rising cloud of dust choked him. Bystanders were firing after the retreating raiders.

Edsel lifted his gun, paused; a waste of time, he decided. This was a chance to track one of the gangs to their lair. He had to get a posse organized.

He heard a shot, close at hand, then felt something punch him in the back. As the ground came up to meet him, his eyes clouded and all feeling left him . . .

Hoofbeats drummed a tattoo and revolvers cracked as the gang galloped down Main Street, gripping sacks of loot. Dust formed a smoke-screen behind them. Bullets whined and ricocheted. Juan was shooting back to discourage pursuit.

They reached the edge of town and headed southwest across the plain.

Kelly called, 'Anyone hit?'

Apparently, no-one was, and Kelly moved up front and maintained a fast pace across the plain beneath a burning sun. The sooner they reached the hills, the sooner they'd lose any pursuers.

A last rifle shot echoed, wide of them, and then there was silence except for the rapid beat of horses' hooves thudding on the hard-baked land.

For half-an-hour Kelly held a fast pace, then looked back. There was no sign of a posse taking off after them.

She pulled on her reins. 'Let the horses set the pace — we're well ahead.' She felt confident that nobody could catch them now.

The gang was jubilant. They'd got away with most of the bank's money, and no-one was chasing them.

'Easy pickings,' Griff said.

'Man, the easiest,' Rafe agreed, grinning broadly.

They rode on into the hills, climbing a winding track, that would eventually bring them to the hidden valley they made their hideout. High up, they rested the horses and watched their back trail.

Kelly lit a cheroot and commented, 'No attempt at pursuit. Don't you find that just a little bit odd?'

'*Por nada*,' Juan said contemptuously. 'They are afraid of us.'

'Edsel must have been asleep,' Kelly said.

Presently they rode on again, following a trail through wooded hills, shaded from the sun by leafy branches, and came in sight of a twisted spire of reddish rock. Beyond lay a narrow gorge with high rock walls, the floor sloping down. At the bottom, the gorge opened into a well-grassed and watered valley.

Recognizing home, the horses broke into a trot. The valley was some thirty miles long but only three wide, completely secluded by towering red rock and fir and spruce trees.

They pulled up at a group of log shacks beside a creek, dismounted and turned the horses into a corral.

Kelly supervised the carrying of the sacks into the main hut, where coins and notes were tipped onto a rough pine table. The loot was sorted and counted and divided up, all eyes watching avidly as she made the count.

Kelly took the biggest cut for herself, sacked it and tied the neck. 'Everyone happy?'

There was a chorus of approval.

'*Si*,' Juan purred. 'I like you, Kelly — and not just for your brains.' He cast his sombrero onto the table and made a grab for her, lust gleaming in his dark eyes.

'Now I shall reward you, *señora*. I, personally, will make you the happiest woman in all the world.'

Kelly knocked his hands away.

'Not now, fella — I'm not in the mood.' Her voice was cold as winter ice. 'And remember in future, I do the picking, not you.'

She slung the sack over her shoulder, turned her back and walked through the door. She walked to her own hut, went in and closed the door, alone.

Juan watched her go, seething with frustration. Turned down before the rest of the gang, his macho pride was hurt.

Behind him, someone laughed. Juan whirled about, his expression mean as a rattlesnake, but all the faces were suddenly blank.

7

After a late breakfast, Savage reclined in a chair on the boardwalk outside the hotel, conserving his energy and watching the action — or lack of it — on Main Street. He was waiting for Garrison to make his move.

Buildings shimmered as the heated air rose; even the dust was bleached white, thick as sand on a seashore, and the reflected glare of the sun made his eyes ache. He tipped his Stetson forward.

Along the street, nothing stirred, not even a dog. No-one went into or came out of Hopper's store, and that was odd; the general store was central to life in the town during daylight hours. It seemed that Calico was well on the way to becoming a ghost town.

Savage roused himself. The amount of stock Mark Hopper carried had made him curious. He decided to pay another visit and nose around.

He strolled along the boardwalk to West Street and crossed over. The front door of the store was shut, and a notice read: CLOSED. He pushed at the door and found it locked. Peering through a grimy window, he saw no sign of movement.

He decided he might as well take a look around the back, and sauntered casually down the alley running alongside the building. At the rear, barns and outbuildings had been crudely tacked onto the main structure; there was a litter of timber, folded sacks and empty barrels.

He picked his way among the rubbish to the back door and tried it; that was locked too. He was rubbing dirt from a window to look inside when an edgy voice said 'Something I can do for yuh, stranger?'

Savage turned slowly, recognizing the voice. He didn't like the marshal. Bick was squat, like a toad and it was his nature to toady up to a man like Garrison. He had no doubt the mayor had set Bick to watch him.

'Could be, if you feel like running to your boss. Considering how keen he is that I spend money in his town, you might tell him the store's closed just when I was going to do some shopping.'

'Guess you can wait one day,' Bick said. 'Tomorrow you can spend all you want. Mark's out of town.'

'He say where he was going?'

'Just on business.'

'Garrison's business?'

'Store business. A shopkeeper has to buy stuff before he can sell it. You ever stop to think of that?'

'Makes sense,' Savage admitted, and turned away.

Marshal Bick watched him all the way back to his chair on the hotel veranda, where he sat and waited. Long ago he had trained himself in patience. Sure it made sense for a storekeeper to buy supplies — but not when his shop was already stocked to overflowing in a dump that likely wasn't marked on any map.

★   ★   ★

Savage stood by the window of his room, nursing a large mug of coffee and watching the street. It was late afternoon again, airless, and he waited for the night and his visit to Anna.

Mark Hopper had returned in his wagon just before noon and Savage had drifted down to the store for a casual look. It appeared the storekeeper had not brought much of a load — and he had hurried off to the *Crystal Palace*. Possibly Anna would have heard what passed between Mark Hopper and Garrison; the whore was his only source of information.

He sipped his coffee and watched and waited. Across the street, one of Bick's deputies lounged in the shade; there was always someone keeping an eye on him now.

Presently two dots showed on the

82

horizon, moving across the plain. Two riders coming to town. Savage watched with more than casual interest; visitors to Calico were an event.

As the figures became clearer, he saw there was only one rider, leading a pack horse. Then the rider was close enough to recognize; a gaunt man with a full beard.

Jonathan Webster.

Swearing, Savage moved fast, away from the window. Somehow, he'd have to persuade the photographer to button his lip, realizing he should never have asked Webster to leave his photograph with the Pinkerton agent. That kind of news he definitely did not want leaking out.

Webster rode slowly down Main, mopping sweat and dust from his face, dismounted outside the hotel and unlashed his pack.

Voices drifted up. Webster's, asking for his horses to be stabled; Kramer's, assigning a room number.

Footfalls echoed on the stairs, the

door of the next room opened with a creak of unoiled hinges, heavy boxes thumped on the floor.

Savage listened till he was sure Webster was alone. He edged open the door of his own room, saw that the passage was empty, and cat-footed along. He slid inside, closed the door and leaned his back against it.

Webster was unpacking cameras and plates and inspecting them for damage. He blinked bulging fish-eyes, surprised to see him

'Mr Savage! How extraordinary — I've been wondering how I might contact you. I left your photograph with Mr Edsel, as you instructed — but, of course, you don't know, you can't have heard yet.'

'Heard what, Jonathan?'

'A bank in Fremont was held up and robbed by a gang of outlaws — led by a half-naked woman, I'm told, if you can believe such a thing.' Webster shook his head as if doubting what he'd heard. 'A pity I could not have got a picture of the proceedings . . . a strange land, this West of ours. Apparently they got away with quite a lot of money.'

A woman, Savage thought, that had to be Kelly. And in Fremont, while he was stuck here in Calico.

'I'm sorry to have to tell you there was one fatality in the ensuing gunfire as the gang rode out of town. Unfortunately your friend Edsel was shot. Possibly you can obtain your picture from his estate when you return. Or I can take another photograph, if you wish.'

Edsel dead . . . Savage's brain whirled as he tried to work out how this changed his situation.

'Do me a favour will you, Jonathan? Don't mention Edsel's name to anyone else here. And forget that we ever met in Fremont.'

Webster looked puzzled. He rubbed the side of his outsize nose. 'If you wish, of course. But I must say I don't understand.'

'You planning to stay long in Calico?'

'Long enough to expose some of my plates. Fascinating place — it would almost seem to qualify as a ghost town. But I'm really on my way south. Apparently there's some silver mines just over the border at San Miguel, and I intend to take photographs of the workings there.'

'Yeah. Well, take a tip and don't stay here longer than necessary. It's not a healthy spot for an honest man.' Savage smiled bleakly at the notion of including himself in that description. 'And remember, it's best if no-one knows we've met before.'

He eased open the door, made sure the passage was deserted, then padded back to his own room. He stretched out on the bed, hands behind his head, and brooded.

Was it only coincidence that Fremont had been raided and the Pinkerton man killed? Or had someone discovered his link with Edsel? If so, he could expect Garrison to take lethal action soon . . .

Well, he could look after himself;

he'd been doing that for too long to have doubts about his ability to survive. And he was a natural loner; being isolated didn't worry him. But with Edsel dead, he no longer had a contact to get a message back to New York.

He was completely on his own. So all the more reason to pump Anna for information.

He catnapped till dark, then washed and dressed. He considered carrying the shotgun, decided against it; he'd never carried it in town before. He strapped on his new Bowie knife, drew it from the sheath and hefted it in his hand.

Twelve inches long with a solid hilt, the point was double-edged, the blade straight and single-edged at the handle. It fitted his hand like an extension of his arm.

He took his time over a meal at Gin's dining room, then moved quietly through the shadows to the *Crystal Palace*. He paused outside, studying the interior carefully.

The bar was filling slowly. Garrison sat at his usual table, playing cards with Hopper and the marshal. A couple of armed deputies stood behind the mayor's chair.

As Savage entered and crossed to the stairs, Garrison lifted his head to stare poker-faced at him. Skinny, at the piano, thumped heavy chords. Hopper laughed. Bick eased his chair sideways to give him a view of the stairs as Savage went up.

Anna waited in her room, as eager as ever and ready for him. He undressed quickly and joined her on the bed.

Afterwards, she made coffee and lit a cigarette. He lay back and admired her broad hips, the sheen of sweat between her breasts.

'D' you hear what Hopper had to say when he got back?'

Anna shook her head, passed him a mug and sat on the bed. 'No. They were in Garrison's private room.'

'Aw, come on. You must have heard something. I was talking to the new feller who rode in — it seems the Kelly gang robbed a bank in Fremont.'

She made a face. 'I don't listen to stuff like that. It's dangerous.'

'Say, this coffee tastes bitter — ' A sudden thought struck Savage. 'Where does Hopper buy his stuff for the store?'

'Fremont, of course. It's nearest. The coffee tasted all right to me — it's a new brand, that's all.'

Savage drank slowly, his mind racing. Hopper was Garrison's man, and he was in Fremont when Edsel was shot. 'That's because you're smoking.'

Anna stretched out and Savage began, absently, to stroke her. She didn't respond.

'You must have heard a mention sometime of the gang's hideout. I need to know. I may have to duck out of sight for a while.'

Her voice sounded drowsy. 'It's a valley . . . '

'Yeah. Where?'

'I overheard something once. You go

89

south-west from here, up in the hills . . . '

She stubbed out her cigarette in the mug and set it on the floor.

'Don't be so goddamn vague!'

'I don't know exactly. There's a marker, a rock . . . twisted like a spiral . . . '

She was asleep. Savage felt too sleepy to bother any more. He dropped his mug on the carpet, flopped on his back and closed his eyes.

8

He knew it was a dream because he couldn't move. His arms and legs felt like lead weights attached to his body. And he saw everything through a haze; the air seemed to ripple as though he were under water.

Yet he thought some slight sound had woken him so that, too, must be a dream. He stared at the door and it wavered as it opened and the shadow of a man slipped into the room. The door opened silently as if the hinges had been recently oiled. The shadow — distorted, menacing — paused to listen intently, then closed the door and crossed to the bed.

Savage smiled; if he'd really been awake, he'd have done something about the intruder. But he wasn't. It was only a dream.

The room was dimly lit. Vaguely, he

was aware of a gap in the red plush curtains across the window, and the staleness of Anna's cheap perfume.

The intruder drew back the bed clothes and pulled Anna half off the bed. She was still asleep, snoring. Savage shook with soundless laughter; obviously she had a customer but was in no condition to service him. Must be frustrating . . .

But he could no more laugh aloud than he could move. His body was numb, without feeling, and the room appeared to tilt at a dizzying angle. Then the dream turned into a nightmare.

He watched, helpless to intervene, as the shadow-man reached out a hand to pick up and unsheath his new Bowie knife. Light glinted on the raised blade and momentarily revealed gold earrings and a bristle moustache. Savage's lips formed a soundless name: Garrison.

The blade slashed down in one deliberate motion across Anna's neck. Her snoring ceased. A bubbling noise came from her throat as she slid to the floor, out of sight.

Garrison let the bloody knife drop on the bed beside him. He looked down at Savage with contempt, then turned and left the room. The door closed silently behind him.

Sweat poured off Savage as he struggled to move. It had seemed so real; why would he dream a thing like that? Anna satisfied him, and provided information. And it was crazy to imagine Garrison would kill her; after all, she made money for him. If Garrison wanted to kill anyone, Savage thought, it would be him.

Just a crazy dream. He relaxed, closed his eyes and slept . . .

When he opened his eyes again, the faint light of dawn was seeping slowly through threadbare curtains. He felt unusually sluggish, and yawned and stretched. His head throbbed and there was a foul taste in his mouth. Anna's cheap perfume seemed to fill the room.

He badly needed a glass of water to swill out his mouth. He stumbled out of bed, almost tripping over Anna who lay on the floor. What the hell was she doing down there?

He moved to the window and jerked back the faded curtain to let in some light. He flung open the window; Main Street was deserted, the sun just beginning to lift above the horizon.

Then he turned and saw blood.

Christ! He went down on one knee and laid a hand on her breast; as cold and white as marble. One leg was doubled under her, her eyes wide open and staring emptily. The rouged face made a startling contrast with the pale and bloodless body.

He must have moved her, for her head lolled, half-severed, on the blood-soaked carpet. He saw the huge gash across her throat and the knife — his own Bowie — on the bed. He remembered the dream that — obviously — had been no dream.

A cold sweat trickled under his armpits. Garrison really had murdered her . . . then he recalled the bitter taste of the coffee. A new brand — doctored with laudanum. So why hadn't Garrison dealt with him while he was drugged?

He felt strangely uneasy. He wasn't thinking clearly. There was nothing he could do for Anna; she was just a hunk of meat now.

He crossed to the dresser and poured water into a mug, sniffed it. Seemed all right. He rinsed his mouth out and spat, drank thirstily. He had to start thinking again — and fast. He washed and dressed, wiped the blade of his knife, jammed on his Stetson ready to leave.

He listened at the door. Garrison had made his move and set him up, alone with a corpse. Was he supposed to stay in the room until he was discovered? Or walk downstairs into a trap?

As he waited, thinking, his brain began to work. He knew why Garrison hadn't bothered with him. Killing a woman was a lynching job — he'd never get as far as a jail, let alone a court of law. The mob would string him

up as soon as they laid hands on him
— he had a mental image of the one
cottonwood outside the marshal's office
— and the mayor's hands would be
clean.

Beyond the door was only silence.
Did they think he'd run for it? He
moved back to the window and peered
around the curtain; Main was still
deserted.

Obviously Garrison had somehow
learnt of his association with the
Pinkerton agent. Hopper had killed
Edsel. And that meant Garrison was
tied-in with the outlaws.

Unconsciously Savage bared his teeth
as he decided that he wouldn't allow
this to affect this purpose. He was going
after the gangs, and Garrison. But first
he had to get out of this trap; he
wouldn't stand any kind of chance if he
was found with Anna's corpse.

Well, he was a city boy and knew
street fighting better than any man used
to wide open spaces. He sheathed his
knife and stood listening at the door.

Garrison was likely in the building with his deputies.

He didn't have long to wait. Maybe they were getting impatient for him to show himself. Cautious footfalls sounded on the stairs.

Savage sped across the room and eased through the window. In one smooth movement he swung himself up onto the roof.

9

The roof of the *Crystal Palace* was flat with a raised parapet. Savage lay prone, listening. Each sound came startlingly clear on the dawn air. He heard a door flung open, a curse with a snarl in it.

'Hell! He's gone.'

Then there was someone at the window.

'No sign of him.'

Savage sneered silently; he hadn't expected a yes-man to think of looking up. The window slammed shut and booted feet faded away.

A faint voice complained, 'It's gone wrong . . . have to tell Garrison I suppose . . . he ain't goin' to like it.'

Savage lay quietly, waiting for full dawn. He heard men come onto the street and cautiously raised his head to peer down from the parapet.

Garrison, in shirt-sleeves, stepped off

the boardwalk and took up a position at the centre of the crossroads. Marshal Bick and two deputies sided him, all well-armed. As others gathered around, the mayor loudly announced the murder of Anna.

'Bick, I won't stand for any lynching in my town. You bring him in alive for trial.'

Savage's lip curled back. Garrison was sure keen on looking good.

'All right, Marshal. Organize search parties — he can't be far away. I suggest you try the stable and the hotel first.'

The crowd was rapidly turning into a mob; angry muttering left no doubt that Anna had been popular with the men of Calico. They disappeared into shacks and saloons and reappeared with rope and an assortment of weapons.

Bick took charge now. 'Listen, this is an official posse. I want Savage alive — '

Running feet pounded the sidewalk. A voice shouted gleefully: 'His horse is still at the livery — he's somewhere in town.'

'Okay, I hear you. Spread out and

search all empty buildings.'

Savage watched Garrison walk back to the *Crystal Palace* and disappear inside. He was strongly tempted to go after him and silence him before he could make contact with the gangs. But there were too many looking for him and he had only his knife.

He crouched at the edge of the roof, watching men spread out from the crossroads to search the derelict shacks. The marshal and his two deputies proceeded towards the hotel.

Savage looked down. There was a gap to the next roof, below him. He crouched on the parapet, jumped and sprawled flat, waiting for the alarm to sound. But no-one had seen him.

The next roof was on the same level. He took a short run and jumped again, moved to the far side. Now he was up against the hotel, a two-storey building that reached a higher level.

He paused, studying the situation. The gap was wider but there were wooden steps going up the side, with a platform halfway up.

He waited till no-one was looking his way, took a long run and made a flying leap to land on the platform. Without stopping, he raced up the steps, made a spring for the roof and hauled himself over the edge.

He lay full-length, getting his breath back, then crawled along till he was above the window of his own room.

Bick's voice floated up. 'He ain't here, that's for sure. But his kit is.' Irritation laced the marshal's voice. 'Where the hell's he got to? Garrison said he was full of dope, but it don't seem that way.'

Savage shifted along the roof till he was over the window of Jonathan Webster's room. A knock sounded on the door, then —

'Sorry to bother yuh, mister. We're looking for the kid, name of Savage, and your neighbour. You seen or heard anything of him this morning?'

Savage held his breath, waiting for the reply.

Webster's answer came after a pause. 'I assume he's still asleep in his room. What's going on?'

Bick's tone held satisfaction. 'He killed a woman, is what. Now mind you let me know if you see him.'

The door closed. Savage waited till he heard them move along the passage, then took a quick look at the street and the progress of the hunt; the townsmen were spread out, moving away from the hotel.

He looked over the parapet to make sure the window of Webster's room was open, then lowered himself and swung in through the window.

The photographer was loading a plate into his camera, and glanced around as he arrived. Calmly he said, 'Looks like I'm going to get the picture of the year.'

'I didn't kill her, Jonathan,' Savage said. 'It was Garrison, the town boss. He's working with the outlaws, and he fixed it so I'll get the blame.'

Webster studied him for a long

moment, then nodded. 'I'm inclined to believe you, Mister Savage. Certainly I was not impressed by the lawmen of Calico.'

'That's good.' Savage sighed his relief. 'I've got a plan to settle with Garrison, and I need your help. I promise you'll get your picture.'

⋆   ⋆   ⋆

Jonathan Webster finished a large helping of bacon and eggs and mopped his plate clean with a hunk of bread. He was alone in the dining room except for the woman who ran the place.

When she brought his second mug of coffee, he said: 'I'm a stranger in town. D'you suppose the man they're hunting actually killed her?'

Gin looked at him and wiped her hands on her apron. 'My advice, stranger, is to look the other way. This is a one-man town. But since you're asking — and just between the two of us — no, I don't believe it.'

She turned about and marched back to her kitchen.

Webster sipped his coffee and stared through the window, calculating the intensity of sunlight falling on Main Street. His mind was engaged with the techniques of his trade.

He must, he decided, have his camera loaded and ready for instant use; he'd only get the one chance and he was determined not to muff it. His gaunt frame quivered with excitement.

He didn't know exactly what Savage had in mind — come to that, he didn't know, right now, just where he was. But that young man had impressed him as being efficient. No doubt he was hidden nearby, despite the search being made for him.

Webster knew he had the chance of the picture of a lifetime. Since he'd been out West, he'd heard of gun duels but had never personally encountered one. Now he looked like capturing the moment of truth on plate, if he were lucky. No, not lucky, he instructed himself; if he were skilful enough. Well, he'd practised his craft for many years and now was the time to reap the rewards of his labour.

He dreamed of taking a photograph that would make his name a household word across the continent.

He drained the last dregs of coffee from his mug, paid the bill, picked up his camera and tripod and went out onto the street. Normally he would have been looking for customers. But not this morning. He wanted one man only and he was prepared to wait.

He stood on the boardwalk, looking along Main towards the crossroads; the hunt had slackened. Apparently the hunters had looked everywhere they could think of looking, and still had not found their quarry. There were men with guns posted outside the livery, and at the ends of the street leading out of town.

Others looked disgruntled. One by one they gave up, passing him as they went for breakfast in the dining rooms.

Webster took a position outside the hotel, set up his tripod and mounted the heavy camera. He studied light and shade through the viewfinder. He had a spare plate ready, but doubted if he'd have time to reload; still, it was best to be prepared for any eventuality. It never crossed his mind that he might be in any personal danger; he was entirely concentrated upon his craft.

Presently three men came out of the *Crystal Palace*. Two of them were armed and wore deputy badges. Webster's blood tingled as he recognized the third man; expensively dressed with white hair and gold earrings. Savage's description fitted: Garrison.

The mayor of Calico seemed completely relaxed as he strolled along the street towards him. It was his town, and he had nothing to fear from a raw Yankee kid; his attitude proclaimed that he might as well be in at the kill.

He called as the marshal stepped from a saloon: 'Any sign of him?'

'Nary a one, Mister Garrison. He's

found himself a hole someplace.'

'Well, dig him out.'

Webster waited patiently for Garrison to reach him. Then he moved to intercept, glancing casually about him; there was still no sign of Savage. He shrugged mentally, hoping that the young man was ready.

The town boss drew level and he said: 'Take your photograph, Mr Garrison? Only fifty cents, and you'll get the finest portrait this side of the Mississippi.'

'Not now, feller. I've some unfinished business to attend to.' The Southern drawl held a surprise curtness.

But Jonathan Webster had learned to be persuasive.

'I'll be moving on soon. Best not to pass up a chance of being included in my Hall of Fame. I'll be showing my portraits in all the major cities on the continent, a gallery of Great Men of the West. In your case, I'll even forgo the fifty cents if you'll pose now.'

Garrison paused. 'Famous men?

Waal, I guess young Savage will wait while I accommodate yuh.' He lit a cigar. 'I imagine this is important to yuh, huh?'

'It certainly is.' Webster allowed enthusiasm to show in his voice as he focused his camera.

'It'll only take a few minutes of your time. If you'll just stand there, against the wall. I need the light on your face. That's fine . . . hold that . . . quite still please . . . '

Through the viewfinder, he watched Garrison smooth down his moustache.

★　★　★

When Savage left Webster, he returned to his own room, picked up his shotgun and checked that it was fully loaded. He decided Bick wasn't bright enough to come back to search the room again, sluiced his face in cold water, rinsed out his mouth again and drank. He still seemed to taste the aftermath of laudanum. It would have been nice to eat something, or have some coffee, but that would have to wait.

He sat in a hard-backed chair, away from the window, watching the street. The search appeared to be tapering off, and no doubt Garrison was wondering where he was. Well, he wouldn't have long to wait before he found out. Savage waited patiently, shotgun across his lap, till Jonathan Webster quit the dining rooms with his tripod and camera; then he rose, opened the door a crack and listened.

The corridor was quiet. He cat-footed downstairs to the hotel hall. Empty. But there was a door behind the desk and he moved fast through it, ramming the double-barrel of the shotgun into Kramer's face.

'Don't shout. Don't even breathe heavy.'

The manager's weasel face turned pale, and his thin hands shook. He tried to speak but only a whine came out.

'Turn around.'

Kramer obeyed, and Savage slammed

down the butt of the shotgun on his head. He dragged the body into a corner, out of sight; he'd be unconscious for a long time.

Kramer had been having a snack of cookies with coffee. Savage wolfed down the remains, then moved into the hallway. The door was wide open. Savage eased into its shadow and peered out.

He glimpsed Garrison approaching with two deputies, and moved smoothly back out of view. He waited, relaxed, motionless.

He smiled as he heard Webster's persuasive voice setting Garrison up for him.

'If you'll just stand there, against the wall.'

Perfect. Savage raised the shotgun and cocked it.

'Hold that . . . quite still please . . . '

Savage stepped out onto the boardwalk, shotgun level, fingers on the trigger. Both deputies were standing well back. Bick was across the street.

One of the deputies spotted him and shouted: 'Savage!'

The cigar dropped from Garrison's mouth, showering sparks as he wheeled about, a derringer appearing like magic from his sleeve.

Savage held his shotgun at waist level, centred both barrels on the fancy vest and pulled the trigger. Garrison was smashed back against the wall, spilling blood. He sagged in the middle, like a broken doll, and slid to the ground.

10

Main Street was still and silent after the thunderous double explosion of the shotgun, as if time had suddenly slowed down.

Jonathan Webster clutched his tripod for support. He'd got his picture but, from the sheen of sweat on his forehead, it looked as though he might lose his breakfast.

The two deputies stood like statues, frozen in sheer disbelief. Across the street, Marshal Bick's jaw dropped as the bottom fell out of his private world — Garrison *was* the town, and Garrison was dead.

Savage's ears still rang as he stood over the body, calmly reloading. It was the first time he'd used the sawn-off shotgun, except in practice, and its effect was more devastating than he ever imagined. The mayor of Calico had been gutted like a fish.

The noise of gunfire brought men running from the dining rooms and the tableau broke up.

Bick shouted, 'Get him,' and went for his gun. The deputies came back to life.

Savage turned and ran across the street. A bullet winged past him like an angry hornet. Angry voices lifted as a mob formed.

'Woman killer!'

'String him up!'

Savage sprinted down an alley beside a saloon, vaulted a fence and kept running with the easy motion of a young cat. The noise of pursuit followed him. He came to a derelict shack and dived inside through a sagging half-opened door and crouched in shadow.

Running feet pounded by. Excited voices sounded.

'Sure he came this way.'

'So where is he?'

Savage kept silent, motionless, his mouth twisting in a sneer as the hunt passed by: amateurs! They wouldn't last long on the water-front.

He moved out, dogging the searchers. He knew where he wanted to be, Hopper's store, and angled in that direction.

Skinny, lagging behind with a rope in his hand, spotted him from the corner of his eye. He spun about, shouting, 'There he — '

Savage cut him down with one barrel-load and moved off at a tangent. The chase was on again. Most of his pursuers had handguns, some ropes, and he wondered why they still bothered. Maybe it hadn't sunk in that with the town boss dead, they were merely a body without a head. But he wasn't stopping to argue with a lynch mob.

A slug thudded into a wooden wall close to his shoulder and he ducked as splinters flew. He slipped into another empty shack and out the other side without stopping.

When he reached the crossroads there was nobody in sight. He darted across West Street and into the shadow of an alley leading to the rear of the store. He moved carefully, picking his way between loose timber, empty kegs and waste paper. He crouched down, reloading the empty barrel of his gun, watching the searchers across the street.

A stray dog came sniffing at him. He kicked it in the ribs, went in through the back door, looking for Mark Hopper.

The rear of the store was quiet and dusty, piled high with sacks of flour and sugar and beans; far too much for a place the size of Calico. He guessed, now, that Garrison had been supplying the gangs on the Outlaw Trail, and making a good profit on the deal.

Guessing again, Garrison had ordered Hopper to kill Edsel.

Savage padded silently along the passage leading to the front of the store, smelling tobacco and gun oil. A door was half-open and he pushed it; it moved noiselessly on greased hinges.

He sneaked through and saw Hopper

standing by the window, looking out on Main. He shifted the shotgun to his left hand and drew his knife; he didn't want any noise to attract the mob's attention.

The storekeeper glimpsed his reflection in the glass and moved fast, snatching at a gun below the counter.

Savage didn't try to close with him. He threw the heavy Bowie. The blade glinted briefly in the air before it was buried to the hilt in Hopper's throat.

The storekeeper staggered back, dropping the gun and clutching at the haft of knife, striving to pull it free as he slumped to the floor. He continually made gurgling sounds, but the knife was stuck fast.

Savage stood still, head cocked, listening; pursuit hadn't located him yet. He crossed the room, knocked Hopper's hands away and jerked the blade free.

Mark Hopper's life pumped out, blood flooding the wooden boards.

Savage stepped back, wiped the blade and sheathed it. He grabbed an empty sack and began to fill it with cheese and crackers and cold bacon and boxes of shells. He opened the till and stuffed his pockets with notes and coins; why shouldn't the lawless finance the law?

He took a last look around before he left; he needed a diversion.

His nose led him to a drum of kerosene. He emptied the liquid over the floor, piled cotton garments and paper bags on top, and helped himself to a box of matches. He moved to the window and looked out. The hunt hadn't reached Main Street yet.

He struck a match, waited for the flame to burn steadily, then tossed it onto the kerosene.

He went out the front door, onto the street, sack over his shoulder, running towards the livery. Behind him, Hopper's store began to blaze, flames crackling, oil smoking.

Savage laughed — there would be no further supplies for the outlaw gangs for the present.

As he ran, a shout went up:
'Fire!'

11

He kept running, shotgun in one hand
and the sack of provisions over his
shoulder, head down. Main Street,
between Hopper's store and the livery,
seemed twice as far and twice as wide
as normal. Any second he expected to
hear the sound of gunshots but none
came.

The only sound was a shout of 'Fire!'
that was taken up by other voices and
echoed and re-echoed through the
town.

He reached the open door of the
stable and flung himself through,
startling Robson who was just hurrying
out, a bucket in each hand.

The 'smith looked at him and spat in
disgust. 'I might have guessed — you
bastard — you started the fire.'

And he limped away down the street.

Savage stood just inside the door, in

shadow, gulping air into his lungs and looking back at the conflagration. It made an impressive sight.

Smoke boiled up into the morning sky, dark and oily, blotting out the sun. Hot air eddied, making miniature whirlwinds that sucked up the white dust. Flames danced and crackled and sparks jumped among the dry timber. Ammunition exploded like fireworks on the Fourth of July, scattering would-be firemen.

He watched the townsfolk reform their chain, men, women and children scurrying like ants, passing buckets of water from the creek in the hopeless task of dousing the flames.

He relaxed. Obviously he had been temporarily forgotten or was being deliberately ignored. The citizens of Calico, including whores and saloon-keepers, were in a panic; their town, largely built of wood, was threatened with total destruction.

He could feel sorry for the few honest people, like Robson or Gin, but not for the rest. Savage saddled his horse and made ready to leave; nobody was going to bother him, and he could afford to take his time.

He led his horse to the door and paused scanning the street. The black stallion was restless, not liking the fire at all. The blaze was spreading; even Bick helped the bucket chain. Water was splashed over nearby buildings; the store was long past saving, but the fire might be contained.

One man alone was not fighting the fire. Standing in the middle of Main Street, Jonathan Webster took one photograph after another, as fast as he could load his camera.

A wave of heat drove towards him. Savage boosted himself into the saddle and turned his back on the blaze, riding out of town to the southwest and heading for the distant hills to find a rock in the shape of a twisted spire.

The black was frisky and Savage let him have his head for an hour, then reined back. Calico was a pall of dark smoke in the sky and there was no sign of pursuit. His stomach rumbled and he dismounted and made a cold breakfast.

When he set off again, he rode at a leisurely pace not knowing how far he had to travel and wanting to conserve his horse. He glanced back from time to time to make sure he wasn't followed.

He reached the foothills and a small creek and let his horse drink and graze. As he filled his water-bottle, he tried to remember Anna's exact words.

' . . . a valley, south-west from Calico, up in the hills. There's a marker, a rock, twisted like a spiral . . . '

He rode all day into the high country, among rocks weathered to strange forms, stands of greasewood and sage. With sunset, the air grew chill and he rolled into a blanket and was soon asleep.

Next morning, when he set off again, the landscape grew bleaker the further he went. And somewhere in the jumble of erosion-carved sandstone lay the entrance to a hidden valley. There was no hurry. He let his horse pick the way, the brim of his Stetson tugged down to shade his eyes from the sun as he looked for the marker.

He just kept riding and looking and climbing up the rock trail among the hills. The bare trail wound through a maze of jagged crags and sunbaked rock. It was a barren and depressing land, seemingly without end, until —

He paused, pulling on the reins. The black stopped and Savage wiped sweat from his face and drank from his water-bottle. He squinted into a glare of sun. Despite the movement of heated air, he was sure he had the marker spotted: a tall spire of red rock twisted like a candy bar. It had to be.

He urged his horse forward at a quickened pace, eager and elated. At the top of rising ground, where the weathered spire towered directly above him, the ground fell away to form a narrow canyon between high walls. Below he glimpsed a long lush valley, green and fertile.

He started down the gorge. The walls provided shade and the air was cooler.

A voice called sharply, 'That's far enough, feller. Get off your cayuse and drop your guns.'

Savage reined back, saw a rifle aimed at him from behind a rock beside the trail. He considered and decided he had no choice in that confined space. Calmly, he slid from the saddle.

The voice came again, demanding: 'The shotgun — and the knife.'

Savage laid both weapons carefully on the ground.

'Okay. Now move away.'

He obeyed, pulse quickening, waiting to see who he had to deal with. Two men holding rifles rose from cover. They closed in, one searching him for hidden weapons.

'Relax Rafe, he hasn't got anything else — and he's only a kid anyway.'

Savage's temper flared up. 'Don't you call me a kid!' he shouted.

Rafe laughed. 'Touchy, ain't he?'

'Macho, like a mule,' commented a third man, stepping into view.

He was tall and thin and dressed in black and silver. His eyes, under his sombrero, were narrow-set and mean.

'What do you think you are doing here, *señor*?'

Savage answered sullenly. 'I ran into some trouble back east, and heard there was a safe place in these hills. I just want to rest awhile till things quieten down.'

'*Si*? Where did you hear that?'

'Fremont.'

Another man drifted into view, a heavyweight, all big bone and solid muscle. 'Could be he's telling the truth, Juan. Hell, he looks just a baby to me.'

'*Por nada*.' And it could be he is not what he seems,' the Mexican snapped in a cold voice. 'I don't want spies around me.'

'Kelly don't like killing, you know that,' Rafe said uneasily.

'Kelly isn't here, is she?' Juan's dark eyes glinted with menace. 'And who said anything about killing? Just rough him up a little, then throw him back where he came from, that's all.'

Savage didn't fancy the odds; but he liked the idea of being beaten up even less. It seemed he'd found the Kelly gang but . . .

He dived forward, his fist flashing towards the Mexican's swarthy face. Juan stepped back, quick as a rattle-snake; there was a gun in his hand and the barrel struck the side of Savage's skull, temporarily dazing him.

Savage stumbled, and two men closed rapidly, one on each side, gripping his arms.

Juan smiled thinly. '*Si*, just hold him like that. Griff, hurt him — make him wish he hadn't come here. Enough to be sure he doesn't get any notion to return.'

Savage shook his head in an attempt to clear it. He struggled, but the grip on his arms tightened. He kicked out with his boots, but these men were old hands in a rough-house.

'Little spitfire, ain't he?' Rafe said admiringly.

Griff, the big man, stepped forward, moving slowly. He threw one fist, then the other, in a monotonous rhythm. His fists were like rocks as they slammed into Savage's head, chest and stomach. After the first stomach punch, he couldn't even roll with the blows.

He sagged, allowing his full weight to be carried by the men holding him, keeping his chin down. The granite fists kept coming, hard, slow and deliberate; it was like being pounded by a mechanical sledge-hammer. He was dizzy and felt sick in his gut; every breath he drew in was torture to his lungs. His muscles ached, and pain hung like a bloody shroud before his eyes.

The punishment continued to Juan's emphatic words: 'I — don't — like — smart — kids. Hit — him — again — again — harder — keep — hitting — him — '

Savage slumped like a sack of

potatoes used as a punch-bag. His strength was failing, consciousness slipping. He would have fallen if not held upright.

He hardly felt the blows as his blood flowed and the relentless beating went on.

Once Rafe protested: 'Hell, enough's enough, Juan. You'll kill the poor bastard.'

'Keep your mouth shut, *peon!*'

Savage was barely conscious, aware only of Juan's taunting voice. He survived only by nursing his fury. *Mex,* he mumbled soundlessly. *Mex, I'll get you one day . . . He concentrated all his hatred in an effort to survive.*

His head lolled because he no longer had the strength to lift it. Blood ran down his face and soaked his shirt. The rain of blows seemed unending . . . Christ, the man was stronger than any ox . . . no ordinary man could go on, and on like . . .

He knew he was fading out. *Get Juan*, he mumbled, *get —*

Before everything finally went black, he imagined he heard a new voice, a woman's voice. Then a dark pit swallowed up the pain and he knew nothing more.

12

'What the hell's going on here?' The two men holding the bloody and unconscious body of Savage allowed it to slide through their hands to the ground. Kelly's voice was a whiplash of anger and her amber eyes sparked dangerously.

Juan drawled, 'Relax, *señora* — we are just teaching a spy a lesson.'

Kelly's freckles stood out on her skin as she swung on Griff, lacing her tone with contempt. 'I thought you were the great fighter. D'you need to have him held while you hit him?'

The big man looked at the ground. He mumbled, 'Juan figured he wouldn't come back if I hurt him.'

Kelly's gaze rested, like a bar of chilled steel, on the handsome Mexican. 'You seem to enjoy giving orders in my absence. Maybe you'd like me to move over so you can run the outfit permanently?'

The Winchester .44 she carried was half-lifted, pointing at him.

Juan moistened his lips, protesting: 'That is not so, Kelly. I know I haven't got your brains.'

'Then maybe you should leave me to take the decisions around here.'

Rafe said, 'The kid said he was wanted back east, and was looking for a hideout.'

'And it could be he spoke the truth.'

Kelly looked down at the unmoving form on the ground. Young and wiry, his baby-face a mask of blood and bruises, he didn't look any kind of a threat to anybody.

'I didn't hear him whining,' she commented. 'I wonder if any of you could take a beating and stay silent? Maybe the kid's tougher than the lot of you he-men.'

She lit a cheroot, sucked on it till the end glowed red. 'Okay, load him onto his horse and move him down to camp.'

'What're you going to do with him?' the big Mexican challenged.

'Is it any of your business what I do with him?'

She watched jealousy show in Juan's eyes and smiled the cruel smile of a cat. She could always needle Juan by showing interest in another man — especially one he'd taken a dislike to.

Still smiling, she swung into her saddle and called softly, 'Come to me, Juan.'

Reluctantly the Mexican moved towards her, wondering what was coming. Suddenly, unexpectedly she stabbed the red-hot end of her cheroot into his face, mashing it out with a vicious twist of her wrist. Juan howled with pain and stumbled backwards, swearing.

Rafe started down the gorge leading the black stallion with the unconscious body of Savage lashed across the saddle.

Kelly followed, satisfied. 'Remember, Juan, you're wearing my brand!'

★　★　★

Savage recovered slowly from his beating; his body was a mass of bruises and his muscles ached every time he moved. Sleep was the only relief. He was conscious intermittently and, each time he woke, there seemed to be gaps in his memory.

He had a hazy recollection of a red-haired woman mothering him between blackouts.

Gradually the periods of consciousness lasted longer, and he realized he was in a log cabin in the valley; that Kelly, personally, was nursing him back to health. He smiled wryly at the irony of the situation, and kept his mouth shut, hoping he hadn't been talking in his sleep.

He slept and woke and slept again. Each time he woke the pain was less and he felt stronger. He was healing, and now he stayed alert and used his eyes and ears to assess his position.

The big-boned freckled woman fascinated him. There had never been a woman gang boss on the waterfront.

She impressed him both with her toughness and ability.

He was eating again, and getting his strength back. Stretched out on a bed in the bunkhouse, he quickly picked up the idea that the Preacher's gang lived at the other end of this valley and that there was no love lost between the two outfits. They existed in a state of armed truce.

He half-dozed, watching shadows cast by sunlight beyond the open door, listening to Juan, Griff and Rafe as they played cards at a table, when Kelly walked in and stood over him. He snapped awake, wary, as she looked down with enigmatic eyes. She was no longer the mothering figure.

'Figure you're well enough to prove yourself,' she said calmly. 'I hear you want to stay on with us — well, first, you have to satisfy me.'

Savage misunderstood her, till he saw the sly grins on the faces of the outlaws and the jealous scowl Juan gave him.

He bounded to his feet. 'My

pleasure, ma'am!' It pleased him to hit back at the Mexican like this even though he suspected that every new member of the gang won his spurs that way.

Kelly sniffed. 'You'll have to bathe first — in the river.'

'That's fine with me.'

Savage walked outside, down to the river bank, Kelly following him. The creek was barely deep enough to submerge in, and the water looked clear and cold.

He began to shed his clothing, watching Kelly. She stripped without any modesty and, naked, stepped into the water. She was no longer a young woman and her face was no beauty; but she had full breasts and wide hips and suddenly he wanted her.

He plunged into the stream; ice-cold, the water took his breath away and the pebbly bottom made standing awkward. He shivered, ducked beneath the surface and scrubbed vigorously to get the accumulated sweat and grime off.

Kelly climbed out, goose-pimples showing, water dripping from her body and red hair plastered down. She looked back at him, then ran, and Savage ran after her.

The outlaws cheered; only Juan's branded face was dark like a thundercloud.

Kelly darted into a small hut set apart from the others. Savage followed her in and slammed the door behind him. The interior was neat and clean; there was a low bunk with Indian blankets, a carpet on the floor and curtains across the window.

Kelly sprawled on her back on the bed, legs parted, waiting for him. Wet and half-frozen, Savage climbed onto her — and was taken by surprise when she wrestled him beneath her. She had weight and muscle and a lot of strength. Her legs clamped about him.

Panting, he tried to get back on top. It was an exhausting half-hour; more exhausting, he imagined, than riding a wild bronc.

135

But, finally satiated, Kelly lay back and closed her amber eyes. Savage disengaged himself and padded towards the door.

Kelly opened one eye, said, 'Okay, you're in,' and pulled the blanket up over her.

Savage left her cabin and walked down to the river, his brain alert and racing. It was time to start work, to sow a little dissension. He washed and dressed and headed back to the bunkhouse.

He paused in the doorway, studying the scene. Cigarette smoke made a haze; there was a whisky bottle and glasses on the table; card players, and men sprawled on bunks.

Juan scowled at him. Griff grinned, and asked, 'D'you pass?'

'Kelly said.'

He saw his shotgun in a corner, crossed the room and checked it was loaded.

'I had a knife too,' he said, swivelling the gun table-high.

Rafe tossed it at him, handle-first; he caught it and sheathed it at his belt.

Feeling good, he faced the Mexican. His voice mocked. 'How's Don Juan then? That's some fancy brand you're wearing — letting a woman boss you about. Typical greaser, all flash and no guts.'

Juan didn't rise to the lure. His teeth showed in a tight smile. 'If you think Kelly's just another woman, that's the biggest mistake you'll ever make. And maybe the last, *señor*.'

Griff added, 'Yeah, put the hardware away, kid. Kelly don't stand for no fighting in this outfit. You're one of us now — and that means you accept Juan as boss-man when Kelly's not around.'

'Yeah?'

'Yeah.' Kelly stood in the doorway behind him. 'And don't forget it.'

Savage shrugged, annoyed with himself; he hadn't heard her approach. 'Sure, why not?'

She turned to Griff. 'We're running short of supplies, and Garrison's wagon is overdue. Take a ride towards Calico and find out what's holding him. Tell him to get the lead out.'

'Yeah, okay.' The big man lumbered through the door to find his horse.

Savage strolled to the door and looked down the length of the valley, noting the route Griff took as he rode away. If the outlaw were allowed to return from Calico with the news of what had happened there, his days in the valley would come to a fatal end. Griff had to be stopped.

He turned casually to Kelly. 'Think I'll ride along the valley and get my bearings.'

She nodded permission. 'Don't tangle with the Preacher or you'll buy trouble. Keep to this end of the valley.'

Savage went to the corral and saddled his black stallion and set off at a quiet trot paralleling Griff's route. High grass muffled the sound of hoofbeats.

The valley was long and not very wide, rock walls rising on either side.

Trees grew under the towering face of the gorge, providing both shade and cover. He took the trail upwards, following Griff.

Out of sight of the cabin, he pushed his horse hard, wanting to stop Griff before he reached town. The rock path seemed endless as he climbed out of the valley towards the sky, a bowl of clear blue dominated by a brazen sun.

When he reached the top of the gorge, he saw the big man ahead of him, taking his time. Savage eased off, waiting for the right moment to catch him. Presently the trail wound close to a steep drop.

'Hi, Griff,' he called. 'Wait for me.'

The big man reined back in surprise.

Savage wore an open grin as he came up. 'Kelly said I could ride with you.'

'Oh, sure . . . no hard feelings about the beating?'

'Hell, no. You only did what the Mex ordered.'

'Yeah, that's right.' Griff was unsuspecting and let Savage get close to him on the side away from the drop.

Savage's hand moved lightning-fast, drawing his Bowie and sliding the blade between Griff's ribs. He gave a violent shove with his other hand and the big man slid out of his saddle and rolled over the edge, plunging down the steep hillside.

Savage slapped the outlaw's horse with his Stetson and it galloped away. He dismounted, wiped the knife, and sheathed it, looked down. Griff's body was sprawled like a puppet without strings, disjointed.

He broke off a branch to use as a lever, shifted a loose rock at the edge of the drop. The rock rolled down, bouncing, gathering speed and debris. By the time it reached the body, it was a small avalanche of stones and dust that completely covered the dead man.

Satisfied he had covered his tracks and bought time in which to operate, he turned his horse around and headed for the far end of the valley and the Preacher.

13

It was not difficult to find the entrance at the other end of the valley. Savage followed a trail that twisted and turned along the rim of the gorge for some miles, taking his time and staying alert. He did not intend to be surprised a second time.

As he rode along he caught glimpses of the valley below. Trees and thick undergrowth masked the drop for much of its length, and he was not really surprised it had remained hidden for so long.

The valley was a rift in high ground that had opened centuries before; so that unless a man knew exactly where to look, he might stumble on it only by accident. And then would have to locate the narrow gorge that was its only entrance and exit.

He glimpsed verdant grassland studded

with bright flowers, the sparkling flash of the creek as sunlight caught the water. It seemed ironic that such an idyllic setting should be the domain of ruthless killers.

The high ground began to fall away and he found himself between the rock walls of a deep and narrow gorge leading to the valley. He rode with his shotgun in his hand and his gaze vigilant.

Halfway down the rocky gorge, a voice drawled, 'Stop right there, stranger.'

Savage reined his horse to a halt, searching for the owner of the voice. He glimpsed a hat and rifle muzzle projecting from a crack in the canyon wall, and his shotgun moved to cover the look-out.

He sat motionless in the saddle, waiting, prepared to shoot it out. He didn't intend to be beaten up again.

'I'm looking for the Preacher,' he called, and went into his spiel. 'The law back east is hunting me, and I heard the Preacher takes in wanted men.'

A long-haired man with a rifle dropped from the wall onto the track in front of him.

'Waal, I guess you've come to the right place. Only thing is, folk looking for the Preacher are apt to regret meeting him. You sure you want to, kid?'

Savage barely repressed an urge to pull the triggers of his gun. 'Call me kid just once more and you're a dead man.'

The outlaw grinned. 'Reckon I'll take yuh to the Preacher then — *mister*.'

He went for his horse and mounted and, side by side, they rode down the gorge to the valley opening out at the bottom. Here, another rider jogged towards them.

'What yuh got there, Cash?'

'Feller wants to meet the Preacher.'

The big man with the ugly face scowled. 'That so? Reckon we'd best accommodate him then.' He drew his revolver. 'Keep riding, you.'

Savage eased his black forward, between Cash and the second outlaw.

They moved steadily deeper into the valley, a swath of high grass with trees on each side and sheer rock rising to a hot blue sky. A tiny creek split the valley.

Further on, he saw a scatter of crude shacks and the wooden poles of a corral, horses grazing peacefully. As they moved closer he saw hard-faced men sprawled in the shade, drinking, smoking, throwing dice.

Savage remained tense, shotgun lowered but hand close to his Bowie; he was glad to be making a less dramatic entrance this time, but was still wary.

The ugly bandit swung out of the saddle. 'Preacher around?'

One of the loungers jerked a thumb. 'Inside, Mal.'

'Wait here, you.'

Savage watched Mal swagger into the shack; minutes later he reappeared with a man who could only be the Preacher.

Savage stared at a gaunt figure in a long black coat, tightly buttoned. A Colt .45 was belted outside the coat, and a cadaverous face gleamed like a skull beneath wispy grey hair. Slitted eyes regarded him in cold appraisal.

'Let us gather to welcome our new brother. A young one, I perceive, and doubtless full of pride. Who art thou?'

Savage told his story again, uneasy under the stern gaze of the Preacher.

'Doubtless the Lord has sent you to me to be instructed in His ways.' The sonorous voice rumbled like menacing thunder. 'I am but a humble servant of God, yet I may provide the necessary instruction. I accept this new burden — you may stay until my conscience decides upon your ultimate disposal.'

Savage maintained his calm, aware that the Preacher was doubly dangerous because he was a religious fanatic.

Warily, he said: 'Yeah, thanks. I could do with a hot meal if there's one going spare — and I might just have a piece of news of interest to you.'

'The good Lord provides. There is always something in the pot on the stove — you may help yourself.'

Savage followed the Preacher into the shack. Beyond the weathered door was a plain wood table with chairs, and bunks along one wall.

He helped himself to a plate and filled it from the cast iron pot on the stove; it was some kind of stew containing a bit of everything — beans, beef, corn — but it tasted fine.

While he ate, Mal, Cash and another outlaw came in and stood behind his chair. Savage sniffed the sour smell of an unwashed body. He turned to inspect the third man; small and bow-legged, with a stubbled face.

'D'you mind moving back? I'm eating.'

Cash laughed. 'Got yuh there, Luke. No use you trying to sneak up on anyone.'

'Ye should not make mock of the afflicted,' the Preacher intoned.

'Guess his affliction would wash off,' Savage said, and added: 'Does silver interest you?'

Mal grunted out. 'Silver, and gold,

and paper money.'

'Right now,' Cash remarked, 'even a few dimes interests us.'

The Preacher glared at them, and Savage got the idea things hadn't been going well for the gang. Maybe the Preacher, too, needed letting off the hook.

'Yes, it is possible that anything you have to say concerning silver may be of interest.'

Savage finished his stew and pushed the plate away. He needed to get the Preacher's mind off the reason why his supplies from Garrison were late.

'It's just something I heard, passing through Fremont. A couple of men were talking in a saloon, and I happened to overhear . . . about a silver mine near San Miguel, just over the Mex border.'

He tried to remember anything else Jonathan Webster might have told him, then started inventing.

'It's only a small place, so there won't be a lot of guards — but it produces a lot of silver. I've thought about it, but guess I couldn't do much on my own. A gang of us would be very different . . . ' He put a sneer into his voice. 'A few greasers won't stand up to the Preacher's outfit if all I hear is true.'

'Woe unto the rich. You are suggesting a raid on this mine?'

'A raid in force.'

'I like it,' Cash chimed in. 'After that stage mixup, I like it.'

'Yeah,' Mal added. 'Sounds good.'

Luke introduced the only sour note. 'Sure, if we can believe this hombre.'

The Preacher stroked his lantern jaw reflectively. 'Below the border? It is possible, I suppose . . . I seem to recall tales of this mine . . . yes, the *Dolar de Plata*.'

'Like taking candy from a kid,' Savage said firmly. 'A night raid. We go in fast, hit 'em hard, grab the loot and we're away before they get organized. We'll be back across the border before any pursuit catches up with us.'

'Yes.' The Preacher continued to

stroke his jaw. 'Your idea sounds attractive.' He turned to Mal. 'Get the men together — we leave in the morning.'

★ ★ ★

Savage woke. One second he was asleep, the next fully alert. Moonlight flooded the shack and men snored. He had gone to his bunk early with the excuse that he'd had a hard day's riding. He was fully dressed, apart from his boots.

He lay motionless, hand gripping the haft of his Bowie knife, listening intently to make sure that none of the gang were awake. He didn't think so, considering the amount of liquor they'd consumed during the evening. Satisfied he was unobserved, he carried his boots outside and put them on.

He waited in shadow, eyes adjusting to the moonlight, ears cocked for the slightest sound. He felt contempt; the Preacher was so certain of his security that he didn't even bother to post a night guard.

Savage made his way to the corral, saddled his black and trotted away. Out of earshot of the huts, he pushed his horse to a gallop as he moved down the length of the valley.

Stars were sprinkled like glittering diamonds in a night sky soft as velvet and the full moon bathed the land in silver. A gentle breeze murmured among the tall grasses, cooling the air after the heat of day.

He felt exhilarated, young and fit and enjoying the night ride, and laughed aloud; a few weeks back, in New York, he could never have imagined himself on the back of a horse out west.

He watched shadowy trees float past, mile after mile and thought he must be nearing Kelly's camp. He pulled on the reins and the stallion, reluctantly, slowed its headlong gallop. He listened, wary now, for tell-tale sounds.

Presently he glimpsed the dark outline of huts by moonlight; and a voice called sharply: 'Hold it!'

Savage slowed to a walk, then halted, waiting for the guard to show himself.

He said: 'Savage here. Guess Kelly must have missed me by now. Tell her I rode too far and got held by the Preacher — I've only just now managed to sneak away. Listen, I want you to give her a message for me.'

'Yeah?' The night guard showed himself, rifle in hand a dark shadow, white teeth gleaming in the moonglow.

'Tell her the Preacher is riding south with his gang at first light. They're slipping across the border to raid a Mex silver mine — the Dolar de Plata, near San Miguel — and he reckons to come back loaded down with silver. Guess that should interest her.'

'Likely,' Rafe agreed. 'She don't go a lot on that son of a bitch. Figure she might be inclined to do something about it.'

'That's what I thought,' Savage said, turning his horse around. 'Look, I've got to get back before the Preacher smells a rat. I'll be riding with him. Tell Kelly to look out for me, and I'll try to let her know the best place for an ambush. Okay?'

'Sure.'

Savage spurred his horse to a canter, heading back along the valley. His teeth bared in silent laughter at the idea of stirring up trouble between the two gangs — and then sitting back to watch the fun.

14

The sun blazed above an arid landscape. The south-west desert country was one vast expanse of dust and lava, broken in places by scrub or a stand of cacti. There was no shade and they had been riding through the heat of noon.

Savage wiped sweat from his face and adjusted his Stetson, tugging the brim lower to protect his eyes from the sun's burning glare.

They had set out, well after sunrise, due to the gang's late-night drinking — and the Preacher had been no more than half-hearted in his admonishment, as if he had given up on their drinking. But, at least, no-one appeared to have missed him during the night.

Savage hadn't thought much of the Preacher's leadership then; now was a different matter.

He rode at the head of his outfit,

stiffly upright in the saddle of a fine grey mare, a scarecrow figure in his long and tightly-buttoned black coat. Under a flat-crowned hat his face was a carven image in stone without noticeable sweat. He set the pace and his men struggled to keep up despite the heat and their cursing.

Mal's ugly face wore a surly expression and he continually mumbled under his breath. The lanky Cash looked limp as a wet rag as he chewed an unlit cheroot dangling from the slit of his mouth. Luke glared suspiciously at Savage, blaming him for this uncomfortable journey.

It had been a long ride, not particularly fast, as they led pack horses with canvas sacks.

Slowly the aspect of the land began to change; small hillocks appeared with tufts of parched grass and wilting plants. Foothills climbed gently and isolated pillars of rock threw welcome shade.

When they came to a small waterhole, the Preacher called a halt.

Harness jingled as the gang dismounted, watered the horses and their own throats. Then they squatted or sprawled in the shade, eating and smoking.

Savage leaned back against a rock, squatting on his heels, studying the area closely. It was the spot he'd been looking for, a natural ambush. The Preacher would have to water here for the return trip, and there were enough rocks to hide Kelly's outfit providing she arrived first.

He sipped tepid water, became aware that the Preacher was studying him, and forced himself to relax.

'The desert is merely a foretaste of Hell, Mister Savage, but you ride without complaining. You may yet prove to be one of the righteous.'

Cash took the cheroot from between his lips long enough to drawl, 'Waal, I'm more interested in where the border is. Are we in greaser land yet? How much further do we have to go to lay our hands on this silver?'

The Preacher stayed calm, but his slit eyes rested on Cash with an icy chill.

'The Good Lord knows. There are boundary markers, in places. We may have crossed over though I doubt it. Beyond these hills we are in a foreign place for certain.'

Rested, they mounted and rode on, through the evening shadows to the crest of the hill range.

Below, oil lamps glimmered in windows, and a foundry furnace lit the sky with lurid flame. San Miguel lay spread out before them, a small town of adobe in the red flush of sunset; a church tower dominated the plaza that contained several cantinas and a hotel.

Savage made a mental note of the hotel; that was where Jonathan Webster would be if he had arrived.

The Preacher looked down avidly. On the outskirts of the town, the *Dolar de Plata* mine was obviously going full blast. Men, like ants, scurried around wagon-loads of ore. There were sheds surrounded by a wire fence, and armed guards.

'Looks like someone tried before us,' Savage commented.

'Perhaps — but we shall succeed.'

The Preacher studied the layout for some time. But Savage's attention was immediately drawn to one small shed set apart from the rest and flying a red flag. His eyes gleamed: explosives.

'Mark well the sheds,' the Preacher commanded. 'That will be where the refined silver is stored. Rest now. We shall strike like the sword of the Lord an hour before dawn.'

Savage found a grassy hollow, wrapped himself in a blanket and tried to relax. He closed his eyes and dozed lightly, waking at a sudden drop in temperature, the smell of burning tobacco, the hoot of an owl . . .

He came alert as the clink of harness sounded, and the Preacher's voice: 'It is time.'

He rose in the pre-dawn darkness, saddled his horse and mounted. By starlight he watched the shadowy figures of the gang as they formed up and rode quietly down the hillside. No lights showed at the mine.

By the time they reached the foot of the hills, there was a glimmer of light on the horizon, enough to make out the shape of flat-roofed adobe buildings. The Preacher led them boldly through the empty streets of San Miguel. As they crossed the central plaza, Savage dropped out.

He reined back and waited motionless in shadow for the clip-clop of hooves to fade away. Then he crossed to the hotel, hitched his black to the rail and went up three steps into the hallway. There was a smell of peppers and Mexican tobacco. At the desk, a swarthy youth sat with his head on crossed arms, sleeping peacefully.

Savage prodded him awake with his Bowie. 'The American photographer — which room is he in?'

The youth sat up, fear glazing his eyes. He grasped at the one word that

158

he understood. '*Americano? Si señor — numero tres.*'

Savage mounted the stairs, bare boards creaking, to a landing and peered at fading paint. He found a door marked *Three* and opened it gently. The snoring figure in the bed was instantly recognizable by the heavy beard and large nose.

Roughly he shook Jonathan Webster's shoulder. Jerked into wakefulness, the photographer opened bulging eyes and muttered: 'Yes, what is it? Who's that? What's the time? Mister Savage . . . you here?'

He sat up in bed, revealing a plain white nightshirt.

'Listen closely, Jonathan. It's dawn, and I'm in a hurry. The Preacher's outfit is here now, to raid the *Dolar de Plata* mine.'

As Webster came awake, his memory began to work and frustration showed in his face. 'They won't let me into the mine to take my pictures,' he complained.

'When you warn the authorities about the Preacher, maybe they'll be grateful.'

Webster's face lit up. 'Do you really think so?'

'I'd bet on it.'

Jonathan Webster flung back the sheet, swung his legs to the floor and began dressing — as gunshots echoed.

'Do it now,' Savage urged, and left abruptly, taking the stairs two at a time.

He passed the gaping youth at the desk and vaulted onto the back of his stallion and set off towards the mine, hoping to rejoin the gang before his absence had been commented on.

He passed the mission church and cantinas and rode into a rosy dawn. At the end of town a wire fence stretched, the gate wide open and the lock shot away. The Preacher was already inside the compound and Savage headed for the sheds.

Gunfire blasted again, and he veered towards the sound, passing the body of a Mexican guard sprawled in bloody death.

Other guards appeared about the sheds. The Preacher's voice thundered: 'Slay the sons of Satan!'

Hoofs drummed and men shouted wildly and red flame stabbed the early morning light.

Savage swept past Mal and Cash, triggering his shotgun, making sure they saw him clearly — then he angled away hunting shadows and moving steadily towards the explosives shed. Lamps gleamed distantly, and he heard the noise of horses and booted feet running, the sharp crack of revolvers.

He reached the shed flying the red flag, dismounted and tied his horse. He unstrapped his saddlebag, offering up a prayer that no stray bullet should come in his direction.

From deep shadow, he watched the Preacher's big Colt flame as he gunned down another guard. He saw Mal shoot off the lock on a shed door and members of the gang run inside with canvas sacks.

Savage drew a deep breath and turned to face the shed door. Somewhere behind him a gun crashed, a Mexican screamed and the lamp he was carrying fell and shattered; the spreading pool of oil flared up giving him enough light to work by.

The door had a hasp and padlock, the hasp held only by three screws. Savage forced the blade of his Bowie behind the hasp and levered; the screws loosened, protesting noisily. He paused, waiting for another burst of gunshots and then put all his weight behind the blade — and the hasp swung clear.

He took a quick look around; all the action was centred on the silver store. He pulled open the door and sneaked inside.

He paused, saddlebag in hand, till his eyes grew accustomed to the dim interior. He made out a pile of long wooden boxes, the top one broken open to reveal sticks of dynamite.

Gunshots boomed outside, tightening his nerves and making him sweat. One stray shot and . . . the idea was enough to galvanize him to swift action.

He darted forward, grabbed a double handful of sticks and thrust them into his bag. Lengths of fuse were coiled on wall-pegs; he helped himself to three long coils, closed his bag and moved outside.

There was a small war going on about the silver store. Guns exploded and lead whined. He spotted bodies on the ground and heard the wounded moan as they tried to drag themselves out of the line of fire.

Savage strapped on the saddlebag and held his horse's head, talking quietly to it. He wondered: where was Jonathan? What had happened to the police reinforcements?

The Preacher's voice boomed over the noise of battle. 'Enough! Move out!'

Outlaws came running from the store, slinging canvas sacks onto pack-horses. He recognized Mal and Cash and Luke. The gang mounted and galloped out through the gateway, dragging the pack-horses . . . as Mexican police rode up.

The Preacher cursed. 'Send them to everlasting hell!'

Guns roared. But this time the gang had organized opposition and two of them went down. One of the pack horses escaped and was captured by a mine-worker.

The Preacher's outfit headed for the hills, pursued and sniped at by Rurales.

Savage smiled to himself. The outlaws would have other things on their minds than what had happened to him. He climbed aboard his black and made a run for it, moving at an angle away from the gang, travelling fast up into the hills, alone.

15

Savage pushed his horse hard. He needed to reach the waterhole beyond the hills before the Preacher — and he hoped to find Kelly in place. He credited her with enough brains to pick the best spot for an ambush.

The Preacher's pack-horses were heavily laden, and they would have to stop for water before attempting the desert crossing.

It was full light now, with the sun a fiery disc rising above the horizon and the air beginning to dry out. He rode recklessly, racing downhill, the ground flowing beneath the stallion's hooves as they beat out a drum tattoo.

He peered ahead, eyes shaded by the brim of his Stetson, and began to recognize the lay of the land. Not far to go. He pulled on the reins, but his horse scented water and was reluctant to slow down.

He saw rocks appear like a mirage through the shimmering air, the sparkle of sunlight on water.

'You will halt, *señor!*'

With a feeling of relief Savage identified Juan's voice. The slim Mexican rose up from behind a slab of eroded sandstone, silver-ornamented revolver in his hand and sombrero tipped to the back of his head. His plan was going well so far.

Savage jerked his horse to a halt, breaking out in cold sweat when he remembered the dynamite in his saddle-bag.

Kelly strolled from cover, cheroot jutting from her mouth and Winchester tucked under an arm. 'Figured this was the only place,' she said casually. 'So what's the good news?'

'The Preacher's maybe an hour behind me and headed this way. He'll have to stop here.' Savage's gaze roamed from rock to rock. 'Everyone in place?'

'Yeah, 'cepting Griff. He hadn't got

back when we left.' The corner of Kelly's eyes crinkled in thought. 'Can't figure that somehow . . . what about the silver?'

Savage grinned. 'No point in loading myself down — let the Preacher bring it to us. He's got the stuff on pack horses.'

Juan's scar turned livid as he scowled. 'This raid is something we could have done ourselves.'

'Easier to take it off the Preacher,' Kelly said.

'Yeah, well.' Savage paused. 'Fact is, the Preacher made a muck of it, tangled with some Mex cops and they were chasing him the last I saw. Maybe they still are.'

'*Muy Diablo!*'

Kelly stubbed out her cheroot and buried the butt. 'Get your horse under cover, Savage. Everyone keep their head down and stay alert.'

He let his black drink at the hole, then led it back among the rocks where the gang's horses were hobbled. Rafe was with them. Savage took his time, noting where each member of the outfit lay, bellies down, out of sight of the dusty track leading down from the hills.

Juan hissed. 'The Preacher — he comes!'

Savage grabbed his shotgun and a handful of shells and dived flat behind a chunk of red-ochre rock. The sun blazed in a cloudless sky; the air wavered in a heat haze. Hoofbeats drummed slowly, then came a line of weary horses straining to reach water. The men riding them looked and sounded happy — must have lost the Rurales, Savage decided. He smiled thinly; they wouldn't be happy much longer.

Kelly whispered urgently: 'Remember, it's the pack-horses we want.'

'*Si.*'

Savage removed his hat and peered cautiously around the rock. Big Mal rode at the head of the gang as they came down the hillside. The Preacher, stiffly upright in his saddle, black flat hat square on his head, brought up the rear . . . eating dust, but making sure no-one sneaked off with any of the loot.

Savage's attention switched to Kelly's mob, flat on their fronts with guns cocked and aimed behind the rocks scattered about the waterhole. He was thinking that the ambush was *too* good; he couldn't afford to have the Preacher's gang wiped out. He decided he'd have to do something to level the odds.

No-one had their eyes on him for the moment. He snaked across the ground, moving around and back, to take up a position behind Juan.

Mal reached the first stretch of shade and slid from the saddle and allowed his horse to drink. One by one the others plodded up, equally unsuspecting.

Savage carefully noted the position of the pack-horses. Then Kelly's rifle cracked, taking out one of the Preacher's men with a bullet between the eyes. He spun round and flopped face down in the pool, startling the drinking horses into flight.

A fusillade of lead raked the open ground and the Preacher's gang scattered, diving for cover. Two of them never made it.

The Preacher wheeled about, his big Colt booming. His voice rose in a scream of fury: 'Robbers! Kill the sons of bitches!'

Kelly squeezed off a shot that sent his black hat sailing through the air as he flung himself flat on the ground.

Somewhere a man was screaming in pain. Bullets ricocheted off rock surfaces and buzzed like angry wasps.

Savage took a quick look around; nobody had their eyes on him. He raised his shotgun and aimed the muzzle at the back of Juan's black shirt; lovingly, as he recalled the beating he'd taken at the Mexican's order, he caressed the trigger. His finger squeezed and the gun bucked in his hands.

Juan pitched forward, crippled and writhing in his death agony. Savage listened to the noise he made and drew satisfaction from it; he hadn't whined when he was on the receiving end.

He inched away, head down and found fresh cover, took a bead on a second Kelly man. He triggered the other barrel; the odds were evening.

He reloaded and worked his way back towards his horse. Let 'em fight it out now — he'd done his bit.

Kelly's voice lifted above the sound of battle: 'Grab the pack-horses and get out of here.'

Rafe led the rush as they went in to grab the silver while Kelly's Winchester gave rapid covering fire.

The Preacher's voice rose like a desperate prayer to his God: 'Stop them — they're stealing the silver!'

His men rallied, loosing off wild shots as Kelly's gang ran off the pack-horses.

Savage kept his head down and held tight to the black's reins as lead flew. He heard confused shouts and curses, the furious drumming of hooves. The sounds faded and he looked up cautiously to see the last of the ambushers disappearing in a cloud of dust.

The Preacher's men were scattered and on foot, busy rounding up their own mounts.

He climbed into the saddle and rode leisurely towards the grim-faced figure in the long flapping coat.

The Preacher glowered at him through slitted eyes. 'And just where were you, Mister Savage?' he demanded.

Luke drifted up, holding a bloody arm, his face racked with pain. 'Yeah, where were you?' he echoed.

'I got cut off by the Rurales at the mine and had to go around them. I caught up as you were being bush-whacked and managed to get in a few shots — got two of 'em for yuh.' Savage's baby-face managed to convey innocence. 'Who were they, anyway?'

'Who were they?' The Preacher's voice was a scream. 'That whore of Babylon, Kelly, and her brood of Satan, that's who they were!'

Savage stared blankly. 'You mean

. . . Kelly got away with our silver?'

'Yeah,' Mal grunted heavily, coming up behind him. 'They got away with the silver.'

16

The Preacher looked as if he might foam at the mouth any second. His eyes glowed like coals and his lips worked soundlessly. Savage maintained a discreet silence.

The Preacher thrust fresh loads into his Colt and began to run towards the desert, firing uselessly into the cloud of dust left behind by Kelly's raiding party. His chance of hitting anything was one in a million.

Savage put on a disgusted expression as he turned to face Big Mal.

'He really loused it up, didn't he? It was my idea to raid the mine, and look what happens. We were rich, with enough silver to set us up for life — and that maniac rides straight into an ambush!'

'Yeah.' Mal caught his mood and his expression turned ugly. He ran a big hand over a stubbled jaw. 'We was rich, sure enough. You're right, it was his fault — the Preacher's fault.'

Savage turned away to hide his smile. Mal wasn't very bright, but he had the ball now and was running with it. Maybe he'd score a goal, and maybe not.

Savage moved towards Cash, who had caught his horse and was leading it to water. 'I'm starving,' he complained.

'All I've got is some jerky.'

'Can you spare any?'

'Sure.'

Savage was chewing on a leathery strip of dried beef when the Preacher returned, muttering under his breath and loading the empty chambers of his revolver.

'The perfidy of women! That Jezebel shall rue the day she crossed me, her and her brood of Satan!'

Mal, looking as big as a bear, lumbered towards the Preacher. His pig-eyes glittered with malice as he grumbled: 'No gold on the stage. Now you lost us our silver. You're getting past it, Preacher — time we got us a new leader.'

The Preacher stared blankly, as if doubting his ears. His expression froze. He opened his mouth to answer, thought better of it and pressed his lips into a thin line.

He brought up his Colt in one smooth movement, centred the muzzle on Mal's chest and jerked the trigger. A single shot rocked Big Mal back on his heels. A startled look crossed his face and he put a hand on his shirt and lifted it away, covered in blood. Dismay showed in his eyes and he sagged at the knees and crumpled in a heap on the ground.

'Jesus,' Cash murmured uneasily.

The Preacher stared into dirty stubbled faces. 'Anyone else feel that way?'

Luke said hurriedly, 'Not me, Preacher. I'm with yuh all the way — but maybe you should ask Savage.'

The Preacher said, 'Well, Mister

Savage, what do you have to say?'

Savage hid his elation and spoke glibly. 'I figure Mal got what was due to him. Me, I see that silver getting further away from us. Time we took off after it.'

The Preacher studied him through narrowed eyes for what seemed like long minutes, without comment.

'The way I heard it,' Savage added quickly, 'you're the number one outfit in these parts. I assumed you allowed Kelly to use part of the valley — so you can't be going to let her get away with this.'

The Preacher fumed like a volcano about to erupt.

'Nay, she shall not keep the silver, of that you may be certain. Our new brother is right — let us prepare to smite the wicked. It is true that Satan has great power, yet the Lord is on our side. Woe unto the transgressor!'

Cash objected, 'We ought to rest the horses . . . '

Gunshots echoed and bullets whined past their heads.

Savage jerked round and saw a band of Mexican police racing down the hillside, firing carbines as they came.

'The Rurales — they've caught up!'

'Let us ride,' the Preacher said hastily.

Savage breathed a sigh of relief as the gang mounted and set off across the desert in pursuit of Kelly and the stolen loot. He'd just caught a glimpse of Jonathan Webster, leading his pack-horse, with the Rurales.

He placed a boot in the stirrup and swung onto the black, hurriedly joined the Preacher in the lead. He wanted to divert the Preacher's suspicions by fanning his desire for revenge.

'Who is this Kelly anyway? Some two-bit whore . . . '

The Preacher's face was set like a stone mask, and he muttered, 'Kill the bitch, kill her . . . '

He set a relentless pace on the long ride north and Savage did nothing to stop him. Twisting in the saddle, he saw that the Rurales had stopped at the waterhole; they weren't risking their lives beneath the burning sun riding across a shadeless and waterless desert.

The horses began to tire in the deep sand, and it was Cash who finally spoke up: 'We sure ain't going to collect any silver on foot. We're killing our horses, Preacher — ease up, I say.'

It seemed for a moment that the Preacher would turn on him, but he held his temper in check and bared his teeth in a skull-like smile.

'You are right, of course, Cash. A burning need for vengeance bettered my good sense. Our animals must be conserved.'

He eased off the pressure and they continued at a steady gait.

The land was bleak and hostile, jagged buttes jutting from a waste of sand with, here and there, a clump of cacti or a lone desert poppy. A drying wind carried dust that stung eyes and clogged nostrils. Hooves clattered across the stony bottom of what once had been a river; the bleached bones of small animals was a grim indication of the fate of the careless or unlucky.

The sun was still high in a hot blue sky when the Preacher unexpectedly reached for his Colt .45. Savage was caught unprepared. The gun boomed and his black went down under him, pinning him by one leg.

The Preacher reined to a halt, cackling with laughter. 'Treachery is a thing I cannot abide, Mister Savage — and since you joined us, too many things have gone wrong. I have lost good men.'

Half-dazed and in shock from the agony in his leg, Savage could do nothing to save himself.

As the rest of the gang gathered around, Luke snarled, 'About time too,' and drew his own gun to finish him off.

The Preacher flung out an arm, knocking the barrel up so that the bullet flew harmlessly into the sky.

'That is too easy a death for a traitor.'

His big Colt bucked once again, drilling a hole in Savage's water-bottle.

Savage sweated, not sure whether because the bullet had barely missed his pack containing the dynamite, or because of the precious fluid leaking into the sand.

'It will provide me with a pleasant thought to imagine you afoot in the desert as we collect our silver from that she-devil. And, obviously, we no longer need you.'

Savage looked up at the gaunt black-coated figure and cursed as the Preacher waved his men forward. In minutes, the outlaws were only a cloud of dust on the horizon.

Savage began the struggle to free himself. The dead horse was a solid weight across his leg. He used both hands to raise the carcass and his free leg to push with, dragging his trapped leg out an inch at a time and pausing between each thrust. It was torture; his lungs panted in the dry air and each movement brought fresh agony.

Finally he was able to hobble upright. Nothing seemed to be broken;

his leg had twisted under him when the full weight of the horse fell on it. Dull ache turned to sharp pain as he tried to walk.

He unloaded his shotgun and used it, butt down, to lean on.

He could move, and that was the Preacher's bad luck . . .

He stared across the desert. He was alone. He drained the last few drops from the leaking water bottle and threw it away.

He looked down at his stallion and felt a lump rise in his throat. Ridiculous! How could anyone get attached to a horse?

Savage took the pack of dynamite and slung it over his shoulder, muttered, 'Goodbye, Horse,' and set off, limping and using the shotgun to support himself.

There was only the desert — a seemingly endless stretch of sand reaching to every horizon — and the sun blazing overhead and nothing to do but walk. He headed after the Preacher, making slow progress, hate bubbling inside him like a witch's brew.

Heat dried the sweat on his skin to an itch. His throat was parched and he picked up a small pebble and sucked it.

He limped along, his leg a dull throb, placing one foot in front of the other, plodding on. His effort became mechanical, and only the desire for revenge kept him moving at all.

Time passed, but he had no idea how much. The sun was still high, the sky a blue, cloudless bowl. His exposed flesh broiled.

He stumbled on, half-dazed and near-blinded by the glare of the sun off the sand. He counted imaginary cups of coffee.

When he looked up next, the sky was no longer empty; vultures circled, waiting for him to drop.

Savage shook his fist at them and shouted, 'Not me, you bastards — you won't get me!'

Sight of the birds drove him forward with renewed effort. He cursed the

Preacher and devised various slow and painful deaths for him. He was feverish.

The vultures continued to circle overhead, waiting . . .

He staggered on till he missed his footing and went down on one knee and it took too much effort to get up. So he crawled on hands and knees, leaving a crooked trail in the sand. He was no longer sure which way was forward.

Mustn't stop, he told himself. To rest was to die. Had to keep moving, had to reach water . . . cool, clear water . . . had to get that bastard Preacher . . .

He swallowed the pebble and nearly choked on it. He was moving mere inches at a time, his strength failing, his body dragging like a dead weight. His leg hurt and, for a time, it was only the pain that kept him awake.

He had no idea when he finally stopped moving and lay face down in the sand, all effort spent.

The sun burned down on his unconscious form.

17

Kelly sat easy in the saddle, jogging along with her broad-brimmed hat pulled low to shade her eyes. She looked as though she might be asleep, but her brain was active.

Their progress across the desert was not as fast as she would have liked, but the pack-horses carrying the silver were tired.

She was thinking about Savage, wondering exactly what had happened to him. He should have ridden out with them. Had he, too, been shot down by the Preacher? Somehow she doubted it. She was uneasy; something didn't feel right.

She had the silver and intended to hold onto it — but, she remembered, that hadn't been her idea in the first place. Use a man, sure, but never trust one, that was her creed.

Now Griff had vanished and Juan lay dead back at the waterhole, dead from a shotgun blast. Kelly tried to recall if any of the Preacher's gang used a shotgun, and couldn't remember. It was possible, even likely — but Savage sure as hell did.

Suspicion nagged her. Maybe it was time to split up, share out the silver, quit the valley and move on to where she wasn't known. A smile creased her lips. Maybe she'd even go straight — but she sure wouldn't tie herself down with any man.

She turned in the saddle to look back. A dust cloud proved that the Preacher was following hard at her heels. She should never have let him share the valley; it would have been better to have dealt him out of the game long ago. Well, that was a problem she could solve. They must reach the gorge before he caught up.

'Okay, push the horses!'

Dust rose, coating her freckles. The sun struck hammer blows of furnace heat and the shirt stuck to her breasts, sweat running in a river between them. She rode with one hand on the stock of her Winchester, ready for action.

The seemingly endless expanse of sand and rock finally gave way to sparse grass. Cliffs on the horizon wavered through the haze. She looked back again, gauging the distance with narrowed eyes. They were going to make it.

The ground hardened under the pounding hooves, the horses smelt water ahead and showed new life. Frothing at the mouth, they raced towards the narrow gorge.

'Keep going,' Kelly shouted, flogging her horse.

High stone walls rose sheer about them, the gorge narrowed to a bottleneck with a jumble of scattered rocks left by some ancient fall.

Kelly reined back, thinking: time to put a stopper on the Preacher for good.

'Here! Get the nags out of sight — get down behind the rocks. Hold your fire till I shoot. Then blast 'em as they come through.'

Rafe's black face glistened. 'Easy, ma'am!'

Kelly levered a bullet into the breech and sighted her Winchester. She wiped sweat from her face and hands, lit a cheroot and smoked quietly while she waited for the Preacher.

★   ★   ★

He dreamed of water, running water. It tasted warm and he choked on it, spluttering . . . what the hell? Memory trickled back: the Preacher! He was going to kill the bastard, so what was he doing dreaming about water?

He made an effort to move. Christ, someone had shoved him inside an oven; he was baking and his throat parched. Where *was* that water?

He shouted, 'Water, give me water,' but the only sound that came was a frog's croaking.

He felt an arm around him, supporting his back. He heard the faint sloshing sound of a liquid, and his lips absorbed moisture. He swallowed greedily and choked again. The flow of water stopped.

He forced his eyes open against a glare of sunlight and recognized a bearded face and an outsize nose. Jonathan Webster was holding a water bottle just out of reach.

He lunged, and choked.

Webster's dour voice reached him. 'If you'll just stop being so greedy, Mister Savage, you won't keep choking. Take it slowly, a sip at a time.'

It took a supreme effort of will — he wanted to wallow in the stuff, drown in it — but he forced himself to obey. He took slow careful sips, pausing between each, till his throat muscles started working again. Then he drank eagerly and the strength gradually returned to his dehydrated body.

He pushed Webster's arm away and propped himself up, staring round the empty desert. There were just the two of them, and the photographer's horses, the second loaded down with his gear.

Webster began to complain in a bitter tone.

'I don't know why I bother with you, really I don't. I had to leave Calico in a hurry on your account. Then the Mexican police insisted that I leave San Miguel — with no chance to photograph the mine. I followed you across the desert hoping for . . . I don't know what. I must be mad!'

Savage wasn't listening. His whole attention remained fixed on getting at the Preacher. He bared his teeth in a ferocious grin and forced himself to stand. He tried out his leg; it still hurt, but not nearly as much. Obviously the enforced rest had done it good.

He pushed shells into his shotgun, picked up the saddle-bag containing dynamite and walked stiffly towards Webster's horse.

The photographer watched him lash the bag securely behind the saddle. A note of alarm crept into his voice as he asked, 'What do you think you're doing?'

Savage heaved himself into the saddle, felt for the stirrups and took up the reins. He pointed the shotgun down at him.

'Don't think I'm not grateful, Jonathan, but I need your horse. Just follow along at your own pace and maybe you'll be in time to get those action shots you crave so much. See you.'

He nudged the horse into motion and rode away.

Behind him, Jonathan Webster shouted: 'Mister Savage, come back — you can't leave me here.' His fish eyes bulged as he looked at his pack-horse, already fully laden. He couldn't — he just *couldn't* — dump any of his precious gear.

Savage pushed his new mount to a full gallop. A load of stolen silver was the catalyst that would bring Kelly and the Preacher face to face. And he intended to be there when the feud was finally played out.

I'll make that red-headed bitch scream for the Lord's mercy, the Preacher promised himself, scream in vain. His flagging horse faltered in its stride and he whipped its flanks viciously.

His mouth was a thin slit and he rode like a blind man across the desert, intent only on reaching the Promised Land where he would get his hands on Kelly and the silver she had stolen from him. His hatred led him close to the brink of madness; only the satisfaction he felt when he remembered Savage — on foot with no water beneath the searing sun — kept him from toppling into the abyss.

The desert merged into burned grassland, foothills and a tiny creek.

Cash moved up beside him, drawling, 'We're not going to catch 'em before they reach the valley. Might as well give our horses a breather. I don't reckon much to finishing up on foot.'

The Preacher glared at him, but

finally the mask of hatred changed. 'Five minutes,' he agreed reluctantly.

The gang dismounted and let the weary mounts drink. Cash lit a cheroot and smoked in silence. The five minutes stretched to fifteen and the Preacher became impatient.

'A fortune in silver awaits us,' he coaxed. 'Enough to make every man with me rich for the rest of his life. Only Kelly stands in our way — her Godless crew shall be driven from the valley — and she is but a woman, a Sister of Sin. There will be no more compromises. She will be treated as any other woman.'

Luke licked his lips. 'I like that idea,' he said, and went to his horse.

One by one the others saddled up and they set off again in a straggling line. The last few miles were covered at an easy pace until, before them, rock walls rose sheer to a hot blue sky.

The Preacher drew his Colt and spurred his grey to a gallop; hooves thundering, he charged the entrance to the gorge, mumbling under his breath.

'Kelly, I'm surely going to hurt you when I lay hands on you. You will regret that you ever crossed a servant of the Lord!'

Behind him, Cash raised his voice in a shout: 'Pull up, you mad bastard! You led us into one ambush — you figuring to do the same again?'

The Preacher whirled his horse about, a snarl on his lips. 'Are you now challenging me . . . ?' Then his natural cunning asserted itself and he lowered his gun.

'You are right once again, Cash.' He sighed as if with regret. 'I allowed myself to be carried away on a tidal wave of vengeance. I really don't know what I'd do without your good sense.'

He dismounted and let the reins drag the ground. 'All right, leave the horses to graze. We'll sneak up on that bitch.'

With Cash and Luke close and the rest of the gang following, the Preacher moved warily from rock to rock, studying the natural trap where the gorge narrowed . . . yes, of course Kelly would be waiting here, but this time . . .

A single shot slammed out. The bullet whined past the Preacher like an angry hornet and punched a ragged hole through Cash's shirt, chest-high. The lanky man was smashed backwards, blood pumping like a geyser from his heart.

The gang split and ducked for cover as a torrent of lead poured from hidden guns.

Head down in behind rocky outcrops, the Preacher's face was a mask of fury as he mouthed curses on his enemy. Mal gone, now Cash . . .

He was pinned down as rifle fire erupted, filling the gorge with noise and flying splinters of rock. He looked up between high walls at the sky and the setting sun and his lips formed a death's-head smile.

'Aye, and darkness shall be their shroud!'

* * *

Dave Bridger sat on a bench in the shade on the veranda outside the hotel in Calico. He picked at morsels of meat between his teeth with a sliver of wood, and brooded on the fire-gutted section of town below West Street. Savage had done a good job.

He flicked the toothpick away and sipped from a glass of sarsaparilla. It was hot and dusty and quiet. Calico was near enough a ghost town, he reflected; those that hadn't already left were packing to leave. Robson and Gin, who had filled him in on the action here had gone. Soon it would be time for him to go. It was unlikely there was anything more to learn — and if Savage made contact again it would most likely be at Fremont.

Well, he had a posse ready to ride when — *if* — he got word.

Bridger had been sent west by Mister Allan, personally, to handle the investigation and bring in Edsel's killer. Pinkerton couldn't afford to let any gang get away with the murder of one of his operatives.

In Fremont he'd learnt that Edsel had been back-shot when Kelly's gang had raided the bank. Learnt too — Bridger scowled at the stupidity of it — that Savage had got himself photographed and had his picture left with Edsel. Advertising himself . . .

So he'd followed the trail to Calico to find the town half burnt down and the crooked town boss gut-shot by young Savage. Well, Bridger reflected, reliving those moments on a New York dock early one morning, he'd named him exactly.

Grudgingly, he admitted that Mister Allan had been right about the kid; he hadn't thought so then. Savage was just right for this job. He'd ferreted out Garrison and eliminated him; burnt down the store so there were no more easy supplies for the trail gangs. And Garrison's hangers on had drifted away like chaff before the wind.

Yeah, Calico was finished; an air of dereliction hung over what was left of the town, silent and dusty as a grave. He'd be glad to get back to the streets of New York — but first he had to nail Edsel's killer.

According to the smith, Savage had ridden out of town, south-west into the hills. The assumption was that he had a lead to the gangs' hideaway.

Bridger puzzled over the part the photographer played. Jonathan Webster had shown up in Calico, then gone on to the border and San Miguel. He toyed with the idea of following and demanding the answers to some questions. He shrugged the idea away. Best to get back to Fremont in case he heard from Savage. Assuming he was still alive.

Dave Bridger wondered where he was right now . . .

18

Savage came up to the gorge at sunset. A crackle of gunfire told him that Kelly had set another ambush at the point where the canyon — the only entrance to the valley — was narrowest.

But this time the Preacher had not been caught unaware. Though Kelly's men had the advantage of the best cover, behind rocks with rifles, the Preacher's gang was not totally disorganized. They too were lying flat and shooting back. The situation looked as though it might turn into a long drawn out stalemate, and that suited Savage.

He reined back, dismounted, stripped off the saddle-bag containing the dynamite and coils of fuse and took hold of his shotgun. He turned Webster's horse loose and hid the dynamite and gun. Then, keeping low and darting from rock to rock, he snaked his way forward.

He wanted to take a look at the gangs' exact position before he put the final part of his plan in motion. There must be no error now that they were set on exterminating each other.

He drew his knife and eased forward, covering ground quickly. Lead ricocheted and whined overhead. He saw the dead body of Cash, rifle in hand. Savage took the Sharps and loosed off a shot in the general direction of Kelly's gang. He didn't bother to aim; his action was purely one of protective colouring.

As he inched forward, Luke spotted him from the corner of his eye and turned, lifting a revolver.

'You! How — '

Savage lunged forward. The blade of his Bowie slid between Luke's ribs and penetrated to the heart. He jerked once, then fell back.

Savage wiped blood from his knife and sheathed it. He fired another shot towards distant rocks; then, nose wrinkling at the smell, fumbled in

Luke's pockets and pulled out a box of sulphur matches.

He lay quietly, studying the scene. The setting sun threw a rosy light on tall cliffs rearing to a darkening sky so they appeared to be bathed in blood. Below, the jagged outlines of rocks showed as ominous shadows. The narrow entrance to the valley was a black hole in the background.

Presumably the Preacher was waiting for full dark before he closed in. Would Kelly retreat? Not likely, Savage decided; not when she commanded the only way into the valley and anyone advancing towards her could be considered an enemy. No, she'd sit tight.

Satisfied that he understood the situation, he waited for the right moment — a brisk exchange of gunfire — and then backed away to reclaim his saddle-bag.

Somewhere in the gloom behind him, the Preacher's voice ranted on: 'Slay the whoresons . . . take the woman alive!'

Savage reached the saddle-bag and

fastened it securely to his back. He moved swiftly to the gorge wall, seeking a place where the high rim was markedly lower. He considered taking the shotgun with him, but decided he couldn't manage it. He stashed the gun in a safe place and began to climb.

He found the climb more difficult than he'd imagined. The wall was sheer and crumbly. He went up, fingers clawing for holds, feet groping for any crack to wedge the toes of his boots in. He soon had to pause; his injured leg had not fully recovered and began to bother him. It felt weak, as though it might not support his weight, and the pain was getting worse.

While he rested, he looked down. He was high enough to get a panoramic view of the gorge in the last rays of the setting sun. Shadows darkened the ground and the Preacher's men were like ants crouched behind black humps. Red flame stabbed the twilight and gunshots echoed between rock walls, reverberating like a roll on drums.

The Preacher's voice rose to him: 'Smite the enemy with all thy might. Woe unto the sinful!'

Savage forced himself to go on, boosting himself up the face of the cliff. His boots scraped the wall, dislodging loose pieces. Higher and higher he climbed, scrabbling for a grip in each tiny crevice.

A wind started to moan through the gorge, threatening to tear him from his perch. Sweat froze to his body. The pack on his back seemed a dead weight, but he refused even to consider giving up. Stubbornly he kept on until, nearing exhaustion, he reached a narrow ledge where he could rest his throbbing leg.

Far below, he could just make out Kelly's gang — red stabs of flame shooting from behind dark rocks. Savage watched with satisfaction; each outlaw gang was doing his job for him, decimating the other.

He laughed silently as he continued his climb, fingers probing upward for fissures and projections, boots feeling for toe-holds. The rock face was treacherous. One foot skidded off a spur of rock and he hung suspended by his hands, wrists and arms taking his full weight.

In the darkness he hung at arm's length, scrabbling with his good leg for a foothold. His breath rasped and his shoulder sockets were on fire with agony.

The toe of his boot finally located a purchase and he rested briefly before pulling himself up. He went up the last few yards, hand over hand, till his fingers hooked over the rim of the precipice. Strength flagging, he had to exert all his willpower to haul himself over the edge. Then he collapsed face down on bare rock.

He lay there for a full ten minutes, getting his breath back, regaining control of his trembling muscles. He stood up, tested his leg, and walked along the top of the gorge, peering down into darkness.

He positioned himself directly above the tell-tale gun-flames and studied the rock face, taking deep breaths to steady his nerves.

Shrugging off his saddle-bag, he took out the sticks of dynamite and coils of fuse, and checked that he had the box of matches in a handy pocket.

Then he lowered himself over the edge, feeling for open cracks in the rock face. He jammed the first sticks in and attached the end of one length of fuse.

The crack of rifle fire echoed through the gorge as he moved along a few yards and repeated the action; and again a third time. Satisfied that the dynamite was securely wedged, he backed off, the three lengths of fuse trailing out behind him.

From the rim, he looked down on the miniature battlefield, then struck a match and lit his fuses. Pausing only long enough to make sure that each fuse was burning, he turned back from the edge and dropped flat in a hollow in the ground.

The seconds dragged out, each one seeming like a minute. Savage, head down, wondered what had gone wrong. Had the fuse fizzled out? He forced himself to wait; it could be suicidal to return to the rim of the gorge if they were still burning.

He began to count slowly: 'One . . . two . . . three . . . thirty-one . . . thirty-two . . . thirty — '

The ground rocked. A triple explosion deafened him. Dust rose in a cloud, smothering and choking him. He heard an ominous rumble like the sound of thunder, and a man shouting an alarm.

There was the long drawn-out sound of rock sliding, gathering up loose debris as it fell, building into an avalanche as the gorge wall split and collapsed. The noise seemed to go on forever. The ground shook again and went on shaking as rocks and boulders hit the bottom of the gorge. He heard screams through the wall of dust.

Eventually he arose and moved

cautiously to the new edge of the precipice. He couldn't see much detail through the twilight and dust, but what he could make out impressed him.

There must have been a lot of loose rock waiting for the right impetus to shake it free — and he realized just how lucky he had been on the climb up. As far as he could tell, the narrow entrance to the valley was completely blocked, burying both gangs under tons of broken stone and boulders and rubble.

Pitiful cries for help indicated that some of the outlaws were still alive; he didn't think there would be many, and those few in no condition to continue the fight. It looked as though his job was just about finished

But he would have to check, personally, on Kelly and the Preacher to be sure.

He waited for the worst of the dust to settle, then retraced his steps along the top of the gorge, looking for an easy way down. It took quite a while. The sun had gone and a pale moon made him wary where he put his feet. His leg still hurt and he limped slightly.

He made it to the bottom of the gorge, retrieved his shotgun and checked its mechanism and load. Then he moved forward to investigate the full extent of the avalanche.

It was obvious that the pack-horses with the silver were buried along with the outlaws. Even a casual glance showed he had no chance of getting any of the loot to line his pocket.

He passed a couple of corpses and reached the edge of the rock fall. A strained voice pleaded, 'Who's there? For God's sake — '

Savage stopped to look down at the broken and crushed figure of the Preacher. Blood matted the wisps of grey hair and the gaunt frame was twisted in agony. He lay half-buried under an enormous boulder; rivulets of sweat washed dust from the grey face.

'Savage? I must be — is that really you, Savage?' He broke off, shuddering and coughing blood. He wheezed, 'My back's broken — for God's mercy — finish me off. I can't stand the pain. I can't . . . '

Savage studied the dying man dispassionately, and walked on. The Preacher mumbled curses to his back as he went looking for Kelly. He didn't have far to look.

He found the dead body of Rafe — and then Kelly came looking for him.

She came down the rubble slope, half-running, red hair thick with dust about her shoulders, amber eyes blazing with fury. Her shirt was torn and bloody and her breasts heaved as she breathed in great gulps through her mouth.

She carried her Winchester high as she stumbled towards him, shouting:

'Bastard, you bastard! Juan was right — I should have killed you when I set eyes on you!'

Savage lifted the muzzle of his shotgun, covering her, his finger curled around both triggers. He was reluctant to shoot a woman he'd bedded; in the moonlight, against the background of the shattered wall of the gorge, she appeared bloody but unbowed.

His hesitation was almost fatal. 'It was just a job, Kelly,' he said. 'Nothing personal.'

In his head, he imagined an office in New York, and Allan Pinkerton. And he wondered what kind of future he had now.

He nearly had no future at all.

Kelly kept coming, magnificent in torn Levis and flapping shirt, her expression as fierce as a tigress protecting her young. Her rifle was aimed and her finger jerked the trigger.

Savage felt the slug tear open his flesh. The impact almost knocked him onto his back. Grimacing in pain, surviving on some deep reservoir of willpower, he pulled both triggers simultaneously. The double-barrels discharged at close range, shredding her face to bloody ruin.